# What
# the
# Children
# Know

Copyright © 2023 by Trish Arrowsmith



First paperback edition October 2023

Book cover design by Nihkri@fiverr

ISBN 978-1-961676-57-2 (paperback)
ISBN 978-1-961676-56-5 (ebook)

www.trisharrowsmithauthor.com

For Anthony

We don't see each other often, but somehow, you
find a way to remind me every day that people
can do whatever they put their mind to.

# Chapter 1

## The Beginning…or the End

Holly wasn't expecting the knock on the door and she certainly wasn't prepared to see who was on the other side of it. She opened the front door and her jaw dropped. Her sister stood on the front porch, staring at her. After twenty years without any communication, Monica was the last person she expected to see.

Without so much as a greeting, Monica pushed a child toward the door. "This is my daughter, Paige. I need you to watch her for a while." She was already half-way down the driveway before Holly was able to reply.

"Monica? Wait." She started to follow her but wasn't quick enough. She watched, helplessly, as Monica closed her car door and drove away. She stood still, at the end of her driveway, her arms wrapped tightly around herself. The evening air was cooling and the chill snaked its way through every part of her.

Holly sat at the kitchen table, still in shock. She tried to wrap her head around what had just transpired. *Her sister, with a child in tow; a child she didn't even know existed.* How was she going to explain the situation to her husband, Greg? How was she going to care for a teenager? How was her husband going to react to having another child in the house?

Once Monica left, Holly introduced herself to Paige and showed her niece the kitchen, bathroom, and temporary bedroom, and told her to make herself comfortable. She had so many questions, but she needed time to think. Her head was swirling with mixed emotions and questions, like someone had shaken a snow globe that refused to settle. When Holly showed her the bedroom, as she had often done herself, Paige closed herself in without a word of thanks. Inwardly, Holly was grateful that she didn't have to try to make small talk and relieved that she would have time to process information before trying to pry answers from a teenager. Those answers would prove to contain vital information such as how old Paige was, where they came from, where Monica had run off to.

Since her sister left their childhood home, Holly hadn't heard a word from her. Through a third party, she had heard that her sister was in Florida at one point and Texas at another. She hadn't heard anything about her having a daughter and knew nothing else about her life once she left home. At one point, Holly had thought about trying to find her but didn't know where to begin. Her husband had tried to convince her to stay away from Monica, set in the idea that since Holly never left their hometown, Monica could find her if she wanted to.

Holly and Monica never got along. Growing up, they hung out with separate groups of friends, they didn't look anything alike, and their personalities were complete opposites. Holly always excelled in school, had friends their parents trusted, made curfew, and fulfilled her responsibilities. Monica took a different approach to things. She never did homework, stayed out hours past curfew, if she came home at all, and argued with their parents constantly, despising every type of authority figure.

Now, Holly had a loving husband, a successful career, a young child, and a beautiful, large, suburban home. Most would classify her family as the cliched husband, wife, 2.5 children, white picket fence type. She was okay with that as both she and her husband worked hard to be able to afford the semi-luxurious lifestyle they lived. Holly worked as the administrative assistant to the CEO in a billion-dollar real estate company and her husband was a partner in an accounting firm. They had done well for themselves, but they also sacrificed a lot at the beginning of their relationship.

Holly got up from the table and began pulling ingredients out of the cabinets and refrigerator. She planned to make a quick meal tonight but now she figured it would be easy to make something that took a bit longer to cook. She had to break the news to her husband sometime and she had to do it before they sat down to eat dinner with their guest. She was secretly crossing her fingers that Paige would stay locked in the guest room until she called her down to eat. She wanted a chance to explain before she had to introduce Paige as their niece.

She was struggling with her emotions. She was mad at her sister, just as she had been all those years ago when she walked out of their lives, she was angry that she showed up and dumped her daughter on the doorstep with nothing more than a threadbare suitcase and no explanation. She was scared to tell Greg, she felt sad for Paige even though she had never met her before. Thinking about her own daughter, she couldn't fathom how someone could be so cold and careless toward their own child. She gave Monica credit for at least bringing her to a place where she would be with family rather than dropping her with a stranger or an acquaintance. Regardless of their past, Holly would set everything aside if Monica were in trouble. She would have taken her in if she needed a place to stay, helped her in any way she was able. But Monica didn't give her that option.

Holly and Greg lived in an Elizabethan tudor and had completely renovated the interior before they moved in. The kitchen was Holly's favorite room in the house. She had large, cherry cabinets, marble counter tops, and a butcher's block in the middle. The eight-burner stove and double oven were her favorite pieces. She loved her job but while she was in the kitchen cooking meals for the family, she often dreamed of owning her own catering business. The more elaborate the meals, the better, even for the three of them. She chose to spend as much time in that room as possible.

She hadn't had a chance to get dinner in the oven when she heard Greg come through the front door. She took a few deep breaths and exhaled slowly with each one, trying to make herself believe everything was okay. She wanted to put on a brave front for when her husband walked into the room, not make it obvious that something was happening. Normally, if something were bothering her, she could keep it together until she got home where she felt safe to cry or scream, her home was her comfort area, the place she felt safe. But she was home and it was much harder to keep her emotions in check. Finding out she had a niece was not earth-shattering news, but her taking up a temporary residence in their home was enough to flip Holly's world upside down. It wasn't her presence, it was all the unknowns that came with it, and Holly didn't know how to manage it. Her mind had already started going to insignificant places like the fact that it was October and Paige should be in school. Did she go to school? Did Monica pull her out? Would people be calling around looking for her? Did anyone know she was there? She didn't have any answers and the questions kept coming.

Greg walked up behind her and wrapped his arms around her waist as he did every day. He had no idea how much his daily routine was going to change, dependent on how long their guest would be staying. Holly expected her sister to appear again in a few days, a week tops, and claim her daughter, only to disappear once more without as much as a thank you for watching her. Greg leaned over her shoulder, kissed her cheek, and turned his attention to see what she was making for dinner.

"How was your day?"

"Hello to you, too. It was fine." She smiled at him, fighting back the tears that were threatening to form in her eyes. "It'll be a while before dinner is ready. You might want to grab a snack."

"Are you okay? You seem a bit anxious." He ran his hands up her back and rested them on her shoulders. "Tense, even."

She should have known he would see straight through her act; he always did. No matter how hard she tried, she could never hide her true feelings from him. "Grab a snack and sit down. I'll have this in the oven in a minute and then I need to talk to you about my day. To be honest, what I have to tell you effects all three of us and I'm a bit distraught over the whole thing."

"You didn't get fired, did you?" He winked at her and pulled a banana from the fruit bowl.

"Of course, Martin didn't fire me. He loves me. Besides, he wouldn't know his ass from his own face if it wasn't for me." She genuinely believed that. Her boss was a wonderful man to work for. He paid her well, was fun, friendly, and he treated her like an equal. But he wouldn't make it through a single day without her.

She took her time with the food, as much as she wanted the conversation to be over, she was dreading every second of having to put it into words. She knew Greg would be the voice of reason, he always was, but it would still be a tough conversation. She looked over at him, waiting at the table, casually eating his snack and thumbing through a junk catalog that had come in the mail. Flipping pages, he was staring over the top of it, watching her to see what had her so out of sorts.

Holly grabbed a bottle of water and sat across from him. "I don't know how to tell you, so I'm just going to say it. You know my sister, Monica, the runaway who never looked back? Today she looked back. She shook her head in disgust and stared at the floor for a moment. "She rang the doorbell, introduced me to my niece, and left. Without Paige."

Greg looked at her and blinked slowly, dramatically, like he was trying to understand what she had said. "You mean, without her daughter? Like, she just left, without her child?" His look of bewilderment morphed into that of anger. "Is she here now?"

Holly expected confusion and a bit of anxiousness about having another child in the house, but she never thought he would be angry. Greg's typical demeanor was a relaxed, a 'what can you do' type. "Yeah. She's in the guest room right now. She's a teenager so that's probably where she'll be most of the time. She locked herself in as soon as I showed her where it was. I haven't seen nor heard from her since."

"So, we're just supposed to take her? Let her move in, stay as long as her mother decides it suitable? Holly, what the hell is wrong with your sister? You can't just leave a child on someone's doorstep for Christ's sake. It just doesn't make any sense. How...why...I just..."

"I know. I get it. But what was I supposed to do? I couldn't leave a child standing on our front step, I had to take her in." Her hands shook where they rested on the table, her cheeks turning a glossy pink. "I didn't know what to do. I didn't even know I had a niece."

Greg stared at her. "Holly? I'm not blaming you." He stood and walked into the hall, pacing the length of it, his fists clenching and unclenching with each step. Who was supposed to watch this child? They had enough trouble adjusting their schedules around their own daughter. What were they supposed to do with a teenager? He entered the kitchen again and sank into his chair, sighing. "What are we supposed to do?"

Just as Holly was about to respond, Paige sauntered into the kitchen with her head down. She looked so young, so innocent. Holly wondered what her life must be like living with Monica, if it was the first time Monica had dropped her off at a house owned by a practical stranger. "Hi, Paige."

"Hi." It came out as little more than a whisper. "I was starting to get hungry."

"Dinner won't be ready for a while yet but you're welcome to have a snack if you'd like. We have fruit in the bowl over there or there are snacks in the cabinet above the dishwasher. Please, help yourself."

Paige looked at her with such innocence it warmed Holly's heart. She plucked a banana from the bowl and sat at the table, concentrating on the peel, not looking at either of them. It was clear, like the two of them, she also didn't know what to say.

"Paige? How are you?" Greg was confused by her presence and his question felt unnatural. But what else was he supposed to do? He couldn't ignore a teenager sitting at his kitchen table.

"I'm fine, thanks." She said nothing else.

Holly took a deep breath, needing to fill the silence. "Paige? I understand this may be hard for you and even a little uncomfortable, it is for us, too. But we need to know why you're here. Can you tell us what happened to make your mom leave you in our care?" She hoped it sounded sincere because in her mind, it bordered on accusatory. The last thing she wanted was to make Paige feel worse about the situation.

"I don't know why she left me here. This morning, I went in to take a shower and when I got out, my suitcase was packed and she told me we were going out." She used her nail to pick at the pulpy string embedded in her banana and shrugged her shoulders. "I didn't even know who you were until I was on your porch."

Holly hung her head, unable to respond. She would never get answers to her questions if Paige didn't know anything.

Greg sighed and looked at Paige, feeling a pull on his heart. "I'm sure this is weird for you, not knowing who we are and just having learned of our existence. We feel the same way. I don't know if I should say this or not but," he took in a deep breath. "We didn't know you existed either. I'm sure you know your mom and your aunt haven't spoken in years." He witnessed a slight nod of her head. "Your mom left home when they were seventeen and until today, they haven't seen nor spoken to each other, so this is quite a shock. If you have anything you can tell us about your situation, it will really help. Now, of course, you're welcome to stay, but do you have any idea how long your visit is supposed to be?"

Paige looked as if she was going to break down in tears at any moment. "I have no idea. She didn't say. But I'm sure she'll come back to claim me eventually." She pushed her chair back and stood. Walking away she added, "I can go if you want me to."

Holly stood and guided her back to the table. "You can't leave, Paige. Like Greg said, you're more than welcome to stay. We're just trying, like you, to figure out what we're supposed to do. You were there, you know your mom didn't give me any information aside to say she needed a favor. Could she be in some sort of trouble? Should we be worried about her just taking off? She's not a teenager anymore, leaving you behind is a significant difference from her simply leaving home at an early age."

Paige shrugged. "She didn't tell me."

# Chapter 2

## The First Four Months

"She's been with us for four months. We need to do something." Greg was beginning to get nervous about having their niece living with them. Since Monica dropped her off on their doorstep, they hadn't heard a word from Monica. They hadn't enrolled Paige in school, putting it off to begin with because they thought Monica would come back to collect her daughter. As time went on, they realized they didn't have pertinent information to get her enrolled. They had no previous school records, no immunization records, a social security number, they didn't even know where she had gone to school prior to her arrival. Paige outright refused to give them any information about her schooling except to say she had only been to school in short bursts of time and hadn't been at all in the past three years. "I think we need to go to the police at this point." Greg looked hurt as he said those words, but he didn't know what else to do.

When Paige first arrived, she was quiet, respectful, and even a bit shy. Now, she was beginning to show her true teenage attitude. In a sense, it was a good thing because it showed she was comfortable with the living arrangements. It wasn't so great that she began leaving the house without telling anyone she was leaving or where she was going. She would come home at all hours of the night and she would bring friends over that Holly and Greg didn't know. They tried to be understanding that she was a teenager and they should expect a little rebellion, but they had a young daughter of their own they needed to worry about. Lucy was only eight. They didn't want her around people they didn't know.

"What are we supposed to tell the police? We've been housing a teenager for four months and we thought it would be a fantastic idea to tell you now because we think her worthless mother abandoned her? Think about that, Greg. Do you really think that's a smart idea?" Holly shook her head, finding it hard to believe he would consider doing this now. She had wanted to contact the police or social services the day after her niece arrived, but Greg was against it. He was concerned about them taking her away and he didn't think she should have to go through that. At least in their home, she had family. And who knew what she had been through living with her mother. The last thing he wanted to do was risk the city assigning Paige to another unstable environment.

"I don't know, Holly. Do you think it's smart to put our own daughter's safety at risk because of how Paige has been acting? I mean, Jesus, some of her friends make me uncomfortable. I can't even imagine what Lucy feels about them." He sat on the arm of the couch and stared at the ceiling with his arms crossed over his chest. "It was one thing when she was respectful and helpful, but now that's she's turned the page, I just think she's a little too comfortable. We need to establish guidelines if she's going to stay here."

Holly didn't want to admit it, but Greg was right. The first few months Paige stayed with them, it was as pleasant as it could be. Paige helped around the house, every night she would help Holly with the dishes after dinner. She vacuumed the floor and cleaned the bathrooms. Holly guessed her sister had never taught her the proper way to clean, as grime and garbage never bothered Monica, so she gave Paige pointers but didn't want to push too hard and upset her efforts. After the first few weeks, Holly finally got up the courage to ask Paige about her previous living conditions. She was horrified to learn her and her sister truly did live opposite lives. In no particular order, Paige informed her that she had to wash a dish every time she wanted to use one. Monica didn't cook, and Paige lived on takeout, cereal, or canned soup. She had never experienced a clean bathroom and complained constantly about the grime and mildew in every place they lived. That was also the night Holly learned the truth about how often they moved around and why Paige had never stayed in school for any length of time. This information made Holly question what kind of trouble Monica had managed to get herself in. Was it a lack of money or did she have real trouble following her? The latter could explain the need to drop Paige off. Maybe she was trying to rid her of the trouble that followed.

Holly didn't ask any questions at the time, but the former could also explain why Paige didn't have any decent clothing. She noticed the outfits she put on and after the first week, couldn't stand seeing her niece walking around in rags and holey sneakers that were at least one size too large. Monica had only packed her two outfits of tattered and worn-through clothes. She drove them both to the mall to go shopping. Holly, capable of being able to buy anything she wanted, teared up by the way Paige was acting. She had never gotten to buy new clothes and had never been shopping herself. Her mother would come home, randomly, with a new shirt or pair of pants for her but they were always the wrong size and second hand. Paige didn't remember ever having an article of clothing that was brand new.

When they first arrived, Holly asked where she wanted to go and Paige shrugged. "I don't actually know what the stores are and I don't really have a style."

"Well, then it's about time you found one." She tried to give her an encouraging smile but inside, her heart was breaking for her niece. "Let's start on one end of the mall and we'll make our way to the other. When you find something you like, you can try it on and we'll find go from there." She looked at Paige and could see her hesitation. "Come on, it'll be fun." Int he first store, Paige didn't find anything. The second store they went in, she started a fitting room with a number of pieces.

She emerged from the room with nothing more than a shower curtain blocking her from other store patrons in a pair of skinny jeans and a tunic top. "These are cute but they're too small."

Holly smirked but managed to control her urge to giggle. "Oh, Honey. These clothes aren't too small, they fit. Hold on just a minute, I'll be right back." She returned a minute later with two pairs of shoes. "Here. Try these on."

Paige took the shoes from her and sat on the floor in the same space she had just been standing. When she stood, Holly knelt beside her and fixed her pant legs. "There. Now look in the mirror." Paige did so and Holly was overjoyed at the look of acceptance on her face. "Better?"

"Much better." Paige was excited and Holly was beginning to enjoy the experience. They spent the next four hours going from store to store, Paige trying something from almost every place they looked. They stopped for an ice cream in the food court and were talking and laughing like friends. Holly had to fight back tears at seeing Paige finally relax and be herself. The last stop was at a children's store where she picked up a few new outfits for Lucy before stopping for the day.

When they walked through the door, Lucy immediately started crying, upset they went shopping without her. She loved going to the mall and picking out a new shirt or toy. Paige set her bags on the floor and got down on her knees and hugged her cousin. "Hey. I got you a present while we were out."

Lucy sucked in a few stuttering breaths. "You did?"

"Uh huh." She opened her hand so Lucy could see the beaded bracelet. Holly had given it to her in the car and mentioned that she should give it to Lucy, knowing she would be upset they went without her. Her eyes widened and she delicately held out her hand so Paige could slip it on her wrist. It was a little big but the dangling, epoxy charms looked cute.

"Thank you, Paige." She leaned in a gave her cousin a quick hug before running off like nothing had happened.

Paige brought her bags into her room and emerged a few minutes later, wearing one of her new outfits. She walked out like she was on a catwalk, complete with the spin at the end. Holly laughed. "You do take after me, for sure. It must be something in our genes."

Paige laughed and hugged Holly. "Thank you for taking me out today. I feel like a brand-new person. I feel...pretty and...I don't know...clean."

"You are very welcome. You deserve to feel good about how you look."

Holly thought back to that moment, seeing how grateful Paige was for the chance to feel good about herself and wondered where she had gone wrong the last few months. She knew, deep down, it was part of being a teenager, but she couldn't help blaming herself. She believed if she provided the necessary things, food, clothing, shelter, Paige would be thankful and act in a more respectful way. Every day she seemed to get a bit worse, but Holly refused to give up on her. Especially not knowing whether it was really Paige who was to blame. Holly was beginning to have small gaps in her memory, like she did a few years back and she wasn't ready to blame a teenager for something that may be her fault.

# Chapter 3

## Permission Slip

Lucy stormed into the kitchen, slid her backpack off her shoulder and stomped her foot as the bag hit the ground. "Mom. You didn't give me money for my field trip and today was the last day. Now, I can't go." She huffed and stuck out her bottom lip. "I'm going to have to sit in a room by myself with only a teacher to talk to." She kicked her bag before dropping into a chair.

"Excuse me, Miss Lucy, we don't talk like that in this house and we don't kick things. Pick up your bag and put it on the hook where it belongs."

Lucy slid off the chair, shoulders hunched, and grabbed her bag by the top loop, dragging it across the floor. Once she hung the bag and found her place at the table again, Holly joined her and set a cup of juice in front of her.

"Would you like to take a deep breath and start over?"

Lucy closed her eyes and pulled in a lung-full of air, letting it out slowly like her mother taught her. "Today was the last day to turn in my permission slip and you didn't put it in my bag. Now I can't go to the zoo." She pursed her lips and stared at Holly, still wanting to express her anger in a louder way.

"Are you sure you looked everywhere? I signed the slip last night and put that and the check in your bag. You were right here when I did it."

"It's not in there. I looked in all the pockets."

Holly knew she put the envelope in her bag. She remembered because she dropped the envelope and had to fish it out from under the bench, bending the corner in the process. "I'll call Mrs. Harrison in the morning and see if I can fix it. Okay?"

Lucy had her head down and responded with a barely audible "Okay."

"Why don't you get a snack and then start on your homework?"

While Lucy rummaged through the cabinet looking for a snack, Holly pulled the trash bag from the can and tied the strings in a knot. In the garage, she pulled the top off the garbage bin and gasped. Sitting right on top was the permission slip for Lucy's zoo trip. It was torn into a number of pieces, but the signature line was facing her, completely blank. She set the bag on the floor and picked up the pieces of the slip. "I know I signed this."

She left the bag and lid where they were and went to the kitchen counter to piece the permission slip back together. Pulling a roll of tape from the drawer, she laid the slip in the correct order and taped it together as closely as she could. Sighing, she laid her head on the counter and stayed that way until Greg got home.

"Hey," Greg rested his hand on the top of her back. "Are you okay?"

Holly raised her head. "I don't know. Last night, I signed a permission slip for Lucy to go on a field trip to the zoo. But today, she came home and told me I didn't give it to her. I know I signed this slip, Greg."

He reached over her shoulder and picked up the restructured piece of paper. "It's not signed."

She huffed. "I know this one isn't. I found it when I went to bring the trash out a little while ago. But Greg, I know I signed it. Lucy was sitting at the table and I couldn't find a pen. The only one I had was her purple, sparkly one. I had to go all the way up to my office to find a normal black pen. I signed the slip and filled out a check. I folded the paper around the check and put it in the envelope and then put it in her bag. When I went to put it in the pocket, I dropped it and it slid under the bench and when I pulled it out, I creased the corner by accident."

Greg looked at the paper in his hand. "I think you may just have forgotten to sign the slip." He folded the paper in three, where the creases were already showing, and he could see where Holly had accidentally turned the corner up. "Do you have the check?"

"I didn't forget. I know I signed it. I signed it, folded it around the check, and put it in her bag."

"Where's the check book?"

Holly pointed across the counter. "It's in the drawer."

Greg pulled out the check book and opened the cover. He shook his head, lifted the top check, which Holly had filled out and separated from the ones below, and turned it toward her. "I think you just forgot. How have you been sleeping lately?"

She pinched the bridge of her nose before slamming her fist on the counter. "I'm sleeping just fine."

"You don't need to be mad, Holly, we all make mistakes. Why don't you relax for a little while and I'll order a couple of pizzas for dinner."

"I don't need to be coddled and I have work to do."

"Fine. I'll still order the pizzas; you can focus on work."

Holly went up to her office and slammed the door behind her. She booted up her laptop but didn't do any work for the next hour. Instead, she stared out the window, watching the sky get dark, replaying the night before repeatedly in her head. She had been through this before, years ago, where she remembered doing things that she didn't do, or doing things she didn't remember, but that was in her past. Therapy and her medication prevented these episodes from happening. It has been years since her own mind tortured her.

Greg knocked on the door and opened it before waiting for a response. He slid a paper plate with two pieces of pepperoni pizza on her desk. "I thought you might be hungry."

"Thanks." She managed to give him half a smile.

He leaned forward and kissed her forehead before taking his leave.

Holly slid the plate and pizza into the mesh trash can beside her desk and logged into her company email, ready to get to work.

# Chapter 4

## Lost Email

"I know I sent that file over to you. I worked on it for three hours last night so you would have it when you came in this morning." Holly stood in front of her boss's desk, terrified that he couldn't find the email he was expecting. "I sent it from home right before I went to bed."

"Well, it's not here. Try sending it over again, I needed that file hours ago."

"Yes, sir." Holly left this office shaking. She logged in to her personal email account and checked her sent folder. The email wasn't there. She checked her trash folder, knowing she didn't delete it. Empty. "What the hell?" She never emptied her trash folder; always afraid she would accidentally delete something she may need in the future and she'd never be able to get it back. This situation was proving to be exactly what she was afraid of. She put her face in her hands, dreading having to tell her boss she couldn't find the file. She took a few deep breaths to calm her nerves before entering his office. "I can't find it. The only suggestion I have is that I go home, save it from my laptop, and bring it back. I can try to send it via email again while I'm home."

He blew out a breath while his eyes rolled to the ceiling. "That's probably a smart idea. Go now, please." As she turned to leave he added, "and Holly, consider this your lunch break. I'm not paying to drive around all day."

She hesitated but didn't respond. With shaking hands, she grabbed her jacket from the back of her chair and her keys and purse from her desk drawer. In the elevator, she rested her head against the mirrored wall and closed her eyes. She replayed her movements from the night before and she knew, without a doubt, she sent that file. In the parking lot, the sun was blinding. The air was still biting and she could see her breath in front of her. She couldn't wait for spring to fill the air.

Back at her house, she immediately went to her office and booted up her computer. She sat drumming her fingers, waiting for the older model laptop to come to life. It was taking so long, beads of sweat formed on her forehead, the effect of the anxiety of not knowing what she would find. She entered her password and it felt as though another hour had passed before her desktop screen appeared. "What the hell?" The words came out as a whine. The file she had purposely placed in the center of the screen was gone. She opened her recycling bin to find that, too, was empty. She frantically opened every folder on her computer and couldn't locate the file anywhere. She opened the internet browser, knowing the email was already gone, but still hoping, somehow, that the sent folder in her email had saved the file. Nothing. She dropped her head on her desk and tears sprung to her eyes. Crying was unlike her, but she had put so much time into that report and her boss was counting on her. How was she going to explain it to him?

Martin had always treated her more as a partner than an employee. It was rare that he had to act like her boss and she never looked forward to it. This would be one of those occasions and it was the biggest mistake she had made since she began working for him. A fresh batch of tears burned her eyes and she let them come. Better now than when she was standing in front of her boss.

After she was sure she couldn't cry anymore, she straightened herself up, shut down her computer, and went into the bathroom to tidy herself up. She applied a fresh coat of makeup and brushed her hair, making herself look as presentable as possible for when she got back to the office. Her hope, not knowing what was coming her way, was that she could keep herself composed long enough to deal with whatever consequences were necessary. After the permission slip fiasco from the night before, she wasn't feeling confident that she wouldn't break down in front of her boss. If she wanted to keep her job, she didn't have a choice but to keep her composure.

She made her way back to her car and sat in the driver's seat for almost ten minutes before she could drum up the courage to go back to the office. She took out her phone and sent a text message to Greg to let him know what happened. After she explained everything to Martin, she doubted she would have enough energy left to go through it all again with her husband. They exchanged little more than a brief "good morning" before they went their separate ways this morning and Holly doubted she would receive a reply to her message.

Martin was sitting at his desk when Holly came back into the office. He looked distraught, leaning back in his leather office chair, one hand rested on his forehead and his mouth turned down. He was a larger man, tall, broad shouldered, thick around the middle. It still struck Holly as strange when she saw him without a full suit. Now, he was sitting with his tie loosened and his jacket off, slung over the back of his chair. She knew his feeling of distress was her fault and it was about to get so much worse. She quietly shoved her purse into the bottom drawer of her desk and hit the button on her computer mouse to wake it up. She leaned against her desk, taking in a few deep breaths and letting them out slowly before knocking on his open door.

"So?" He sat up and his chair squealed from the weight.

She closed her eyes, took a deep breath, and began talking. "Sir, I looked everywhere. Something happened, I don't know what. I'm sure I sent that file last night, but my email is empty, the file isn't showing on my home computer, it's like it vanished overnight. I checked the recycle bin, the trash folder in my email, and opened every folder I keep stored on my computer. If you'll allow it, I can do the report again, I still have the original document. I'll need a couple of hours to finish it up again." Her chest was tight and every breath she took didn't seem to give her enough air.

He focused his eyes in her direction but he was looking through her. Every second that passed made Holly's heart speed up and her face was growing hot. Finally, he raised his hand and made a shooing motion, telling her to take her leave. He never spoke but Holly took it as a good sign. She sat down at her desk, sweating, and began typing furiously to get the report ready as soon as possible. One way or another, she would finish her task, her determination not to lose her job was enough to push her through.

# Chapter 5

## Worn and Withered

Monica had been watching Paige for a long time. She would lose track of her for a few days, sometimes a few weeks, but she always found her again. The last time, it had been almost five weeks since she'd seen her and if it weren't for the figurative tether that drew her near, Monica would have walked right past her. Paige was thin and dirty. Monica guessed she hadn't had a shower or meal in at least a week. She only ever saw a snapshot of Paige's life, mostly followed her throughout the day and occasionally watched her as she made her way home to make sure she arrived safely. Monica never stayed after she knew she was inside for the night.

For the past two years, Paige spent many nights sleeping out in the open where anything could have happened to her. She battled the brutal summers when the air was so thick with humidity, she felt like she was breathing in steam. She fought against rain, snow, and sleet pelting her face, soaking through her clothes, feeling like she would never be warm again. She didn't have options. Her mother had never introduced her to anyone else in their family and every time they argued, the answer was for her mother to kick her out of the house. Paige let her cool down for a few days, sometimes a week, before going back. Despite the elements, every time she stayed out on her own, she became more comfortable with her surroundings.

She knew where to hide without the police questioning her and where to find the freshest food. She had made friends with a man who worked at a deli that sat right on the outskirts of the city. When he was closing for the day, he would pack a plastic bag and set it right outside the back door when he took the trash out. Most times it contained a sandwich, or at least the fixings for one, a dessert of some kind and a fountain tea when he was able, sometimes it was a bottle of water. Paige didn't have any way to pay him back, but he told her it wasn't necessary, as they threw most of the food in the dumpster at the end of the day anyway. He told her she might as well get a chance to eat it before they mixed it in with the real trash. She would often hide out along the fence at the back of the property on the off chance that someone else was watching, she didn't want to get her friend in trouble. She could see a sliver of light under the back door and she would watch for it to turn off, signaling that all the workers had left the building for the evening. When she finished eating, all her trash would go in the dumpster so the owner wouldn't catch him giving her free food. It was the least she could do for someone she barely knew who was willing to help her out.

Over the last two years, she had learned where it was safe to sleep but occasionally, a police officer or business owner would run her off the property she was occupying. None of them seemed to notice, or maybe they just didn't care, how young she is. But it did force her to find a new spot to spend the night and while some places made her the target of harassment by drunk people out having a good time, only once did she end up in serious trouble. She found a bench tucked in the corner of a public park, out of the way of the walking path and away from any streetlights. She hoped the darkness would shield her from anyone out on a late-night stroll, but she was wrong. Two men, wearing leather jackets and chains hanging from their waste bands pulled her from under the bench where she was using her backpack as a pillow. They searched her pockets, ripped her jacket, and dumped her pack all over the ground, taking all her loose change, the few crumpled bills she had been hiding in a small, inside pocket, and the pair of shoes she had found in a ditch close to the park. They left her pack, a blanket crusted with mud, and a spare pair of jeans she carried with her. Everything else was gone.

Thankful they had only stolen from her and not assaulted or abused her, the anger at having her mother kick her out of her home for the umpteenth time was raging inside her. She had been in six foster homes throughout her life, each one worse than the previous. The last time she saw her caseworker, months ago, Paige told her she didn't feel comfortable living at the house anymore. Mrs. Carnes dismissed her feelings and told her her foster mother had been with their agency for years and she was in good care. Paige didn't think eating cereal and toast for every meal or having to fight off any one of her mother's numerous boyfriends was good care, but she was a child and no one wanted to listen to her.

Monica had been watching Paige for two days, leaving only at night to get some rest. Making sure to stay out of view but waiting for the perfect opportunity to introduce herself and offer her a place to stay. She started small, first offering Paige a change of clothes and a shower, followed by a hot meal. Although Paige was tiny, Monica knew she could find something to fit her from her own closet. After some hesitation, Paige agreed and with freshly washed clothes and clean skin and hair, they made their way to McDonald's to get some hot food. Monica apologized and explained that she didn't cook, but she was still willing to get her something to eat. She tried her best to ask Paige questions without pushing her away. If Monica wanted her plan to work, Paige had to feel comfortable with her, she had to trust her.

# Chapter 6

## Nowhere is Safe

Holly arrived at work two hours earlier than usual. After the huge mistake she made last week, she couldn't afford to let him down again. He had given her a huge assignment to complete and it had a short deadline. Four days was all the time she had. Even though it was early in the morning, she used the two extra hours to finish her coffee, return a few phone calls, and respond to a number of emails that had been waiting for a reply since yesterday. The rest of her day she planned on dedicating to her new assignment. Every day, she got to the office thirty minutes ahead of Martin so she had time to prepare her notes for him. She had just finished briefing him on his meetings and scheduled calls for the day when the phone on her desk started to ring. It was odd timing since her cell phone had ceased vibrating on the top of her desk no more than ten seconds before. She excused herself from Martin's office and picked up the phone.

"Yes, this is she." All at once, she was angry, confused, and upset as she listened to the person on the other end of the phone. "I'll be there as soon as possible. Thank you for calling." She hung up the receiver and placed her head in her hands. *What the hell was happening?* This was more important than any project she had going on at work, but after last week, she dreaded having to tell Martin that she needed to leave right away. She stood, took a deep breath, and closed her eyes, exhaling slowly as she walked back to her boss's office.

Holly grabbed her bag and slung it over her shoulder, opened her desk drawer and grabbed her car keys, pocketed her phone, and left the office. She was half-sprinting through the parking lot, taking care not to roll her ankle in the heels she had on her feet. Greg had sent her two text messages before she reached her car and he was calling as she was opening her door.

"Hello?" She was annoyed that he was being so persistent, but she knew, as soon as she got to her car, she would have been doing the same thing if he hadn't gotten to her first.

"What the hell is going on, Holly? I just got a call from the school about Lucy and now I have to leave work right before a meeting with the guys from upstairs."

Communication between the two of them had been minimal for the last week after he didn't believe her about the field trip to the zoo. She could hear the aggravation in his voice and it made her angry. *Why would he assume this was somehow her fault?* She wasn't the one who had called him and she didn't know what they were walking in to either. "I have no idea what this is about but I'm sure we'll find out once we get there."

"I guess we will."

Holly hit the end call button and threw her phone on the passenger seat without replying, squealing her tires as she left the parking lot.

They arrived at the same time and parked alongside each other. The parking lot was in desperate need of repaving, snow and freezing winters had cracked the pavement and left potholes large enough to swallow a tire. The school needed just as many repairs. It was an old brick building, the same one Holly and Monica attended while they were in elementary school. It was always a happy place when they were young. Holly remembered, vividly, the walls painted with bright colors with cartoon characters and outdoor landscapes. Over the years, the walls had been repainted and were now a gloomy beige and the halls had dim lighting that reminded her more of an asylum she would see in movies.

Greg didn't say a word to her as they made their way to the front of the building. His face was pinched and she knew he was angry. She took a deep breath, as she had done more times than she could count the last few weeks. She was upset, too, and she assumed Greg just didn't know where to direct his anger. She couldn't blame him for being mad at her. She had been acting cold toward him the last few days, unable to forgive him for not believing her. He swung the front door open and it groaned from the force. He walked through and let it go behind him, not holding it open for her. Catching it before it slammed into her, she moaned, "thanks," while glaring at his hulking frame in front of her.

He turned his head toward her without slowing down. "Don't get smart with me. I'm only here because of Lucy." With that, he quickened his step as he made his way down the hall. Holly lagged behind even though she was anxious to find out what the phone call had been about. She had no desire to enter the principal's office at the same time as her seething husband. She hoped that if she gave him some space, he might calm down before he walked in. The last thing they needed was for him to lose his temper in front of a group of school employees.

When she arrived in the office, the secretary disappeared into the principal's personal office and reappeared a few moments later. "You can both go in now."

Holly and Greg marched into the rather large office that held a large meeting table as well as two high-backed chairs that faced the oak desk. Sitting at the table were the principal, Charlie Lynch, the school psychologist, and a woman neither of them recognized. Mr. Lynch stood and shook both their hands before motioning for them to take a seat.

"First, thank you for joining us on such short notice. I'm sure you're familiar with Dr. Watkins, and this is Pat Mendel." He pointed to each as he introduced them.

"I'm sorry," Holly cut in. "Who is Pat Mendel?"

"Ms. Mendel is a social worker from DCS. She has agreed to…"

"Whoa." Greg all but shouted his response. "DCS? Why is a member of DCS here? What is going on?"

Holly could feel his tension from two feet away. He had been angry a few times over the past few months, but it didn't feel like this. His body tensed and his face turned a crimson color. She didn't recognize the man sitting next to her.

"Please, Mr. Berenger, stay calm and we'll explain everything to you. We thought it might be better to have Ms. Mendel accompany us so if it's found warranted, she wouldn't have to do this interview over again."

"Warranted?" Holly's voice was much louder than she intended. "How is bringing DCS here warranted? And where is Lucy? Shouldn't she be here since this involves her?"

Mr. Lynch put his hand up to stop her. "We will get to that. But, please, let me explain why you're here and why Mr. Mendel is here and we'll bring Lucy in after."

Holly and Greg looked at each other with the fiercest look either of them had ever seen in the other's eyes. This wasn't going to be a good day and they both felt it. Mr. Lynch started speaking and they both had to refocus to hear the words that were coming out of his mouth.

He slid a piece of paper across the conference table so Holly and Greg could see what he was referring to. "I have highlighted the passage that is the main reason for us asking you to join us today. We are hoping you might be able to help us out a bit and explain what Lucy was trying to say here." He threaded his fingers together and rested his hands on the table.

Holly slid the paper closer to them and blinked repeatedly, not believing the marked words in front of her.

PLEASE HELP ME. I AM NOT SAFE AT HOME.

Tears sprang to Holly's eyes and anger burned on Greg's face. Neither of them had any idea what this was referring to.

Seeing the confusion and what she was sure to be worry on their faces Pat Mendel finally spoke. "As I'm sure you're aware, as we are, children may make false claims in the event they feel they aren't getting enough attention from one place or another. Most often, it's due to the absence of a parent, but that's not always the case. We wanted to bring you in to see if you could offer any insight or rational explanation as to why she would write something like this."

Holly couldn't bring herself to take her eyes off the paper lying in front of her. "I. I don't have any idea why she would say something like this. It doesn't make any sense. I mean, she was upset with me last week because I forgot to give her the permission slip for the trip to the zoo, but I called the next morning and got it all straightened out."

Greg pushed his chair back, slamming his palms on the table. "This is ridiculous. Where is Lucy? We'll put a stop to the asinine situation right now. Bring her in here." Holly pulled on her husband's shirt sleeve in an attempt to get him to sit back down. She gave him a sideways glance to warn him that his outburst was not going to help their situation.

"Mr. Berenger, please sit? I want to be able to tell you about our conversation with Lucy before we bring her in." The principal kept his voice calm and even, most likely due to having gone through this scenario many times in his career.

Greg slowly sat down and Holly could feel his body shaking under her touch. In all their years together, she had never seen him so angry and she was glad of it.

The principal began to recap his conversation with Lucy, stating that she claims she didn't write the message in her homework assignment. She swore she didn't and when they tried to press her on the subject, she clammed up and started to cry. That alone should have been enough, but the real concern came when, while she was crying, she managed to squeak out 'I'm going to get in so much trouble for this. I didn't do it.' That statement is what worried the principal and psychologist the most. They didn't know, because she wouldn't tell them, if it was because people would think she was lying or because there was an actual problem at home.

It took another half hour before they were willing to let Lucy enter the office. Holly was worried that Greg was going to completely blow up when he saw her and he was worried about the same thing. He tried to take Holly's subtle suggestion to contain his anger, but it didn't help much.

The secretary escorted Lucy into the office with her chin buried in her chest. She looked so innocent in her navy and red polka dot dress. Holly stood to give her a hug and Greg beat her to Lucy. He shoved the paper in her face.

"Did you write this?"

She shook her head. "I didn't write it, Daddy."

"See? There you go. She didn't write it. I think we're done here." He rested his hand on Lucy's shoulder to lead her out of the office.

Pat Mendel stood. "Not quite, Mr. Berenger. We all need to have a discussion together."

# Chapter 7

## Ice Cream Makes Everything Better

Summer was just beginning and Holly was sitting on her swing set enjoying an ice cream cone. Her mother always made it just the way she liked it: one scoop of chocolate with a scoop of vanilla on top, chocolate sauce squirted inside the cone. It was only the first week of June, but the sun was strong and the scoop of vanilla was already threatening to drip on her dress.

Monica bounced through the back yard and joined her on the swings, licking her own ice cream: caramel on the inside, one scoop of black raspberry topped by a scoop of strawberry.

"What did you get a cone for?" Her braids fell perfectly over her shoulders, curling at the ends.

A smile spread across Monica's face. "My report card was better this time and my teacher said she I improved." Her tone conveyed one that told Holly she wouldn't be able to say the same.

"Hmm. You don't deserve a cone for not being a complete dummy. Are you going to get one for not peeing your pants, too?"

"I do to deserve it." She pushed her feet into the ground to gently swing back and forth, her ponytail flying behind her when she swung forward.

Holly dug the toe of her shoe in the dirt to stop her own swing from moving and stood up. "Well, I don't care what your teacher says. She probably just feels bad for you because you're the dumbest kid in class." She swiped her hand in front of her, knocking Monica's ice cream to the ground. The rest of the strawberry scoop flew in one direction and the black raspberry landed in front of her, cone up, like it was wearing a dunce cap, mocking her.

As much as she wanted to, Monica refused to allow herself to cry. She wanted that ice cream and she knew she deserved it no matter what her sister said. With a ragged intake of breath and watery eyes, she looked up from the melting puddle of purple to find Holly already half-way back to the house, her own cone held securely in her hand.

"Mom." She drew out the middle of the word in an elaborate whine. "Mom? Monica threw her ice cream..." The door slammed shut behind her, swallowing the rest of the sentence with it.

This was how life was for Monica. She knew her mother wouldn't give her a chance to tell her side of the story because 'destructive behavior,' as her mother called it, was typical of her. She kicked her legs high, careful to avoid the sticky mess beneath her feet and pictured Holly inside, getting an extra scoop for lying while she couldn't enjoy any of hers for doing something good. Maybe, she thought, she would run away.

# Chapter 8

## Worse than the Terrible Twos

Lucy sat on the family room floor with her shoulders hunched, her bottom lip protruding. When Paige first arrived, the two quickly became close friends. Even though they had a significant age difference, Paige never seemed to mind having her around. They talked and played games, watched movies and went for walks. It made Lucy happy to have someone at home to spend time with. All her friends had siblings they could play with if they didn't have friends over and Lucy had begged her parents for years to give her a baby brother or sister. Once Paige moved in, she didn't have a need to ask anymore.

Over the last two months, Paige changed. She didn't want to spend any time with Lucy anymore, she ignored her when she tried to speak to her. She brought friends over and they were either mean to her or disregarded her when she tried to join them. Lucy couldn't understand what she did to make her cousin not like her anymore. She decided to tell her mother about how mean Paige was being to her. She hoped she would get grounded so she would have to stay home and not have friends over. Maybe her mom would force Paige to spend time with her.

"Mom, I don't think Paige likes me anymore." For dramatic effect, she stuck her bottom lip out again and hung her head.

Holly stopped washing the pan in her hand and set it in the sink. "What would make you think that?" She walked to the table and sat down, wiping her hands on a dish towel. "Come sit with me."

Lucy kept her head down and shuffled her way to the table, her arms limp at her sides. "She's not very nice to me anymore."

"She spends an awful lot of time with you. Do you think she would do that if she didn't like you?"

"But she's gone all the time now. And when she brings her friends here, she acts mean and ignores me. And her friends pick on me and call me names."

"Well, I can certainly understand why that would make you upset. But you need to understand, Paige is a teenager. It's a very tough time in someone's life. She's becoming an adult. She still likes the same things she did when she was little, but sometimes she has to hide those things from her friends so she can seem more grown up."

"But she can't hide me. I'm always in the room when her friends can see me."

Holly did her best to suppress a grin. "That's true. But maybe when her friends are over, she wants to spend time with just them. Just like she does when you two watch a movie together. She doesn't invite daddy and I to watch it with you. She wants to spend time with only you. And sometimes she wants time with other people her own age. She wants to act grown up when her friends are with her."

"So, she won't like me anymore because she'll be a grown up?"

"Oh no, honey. She'll still like you. Paige loves you. She just needs time away from you sometimes. Do you understand?"

"No." Lucy shrugged her shoulders, slid off her chair, and skipped out of the kitchen.

Holly went back to washing the remaining dishes. She understood where Lucy was coming from, but she was too young to understand that Paige was at a point in her life where she probably did see Lucy as a bother. Their age difference was significant and Paige was entering those awful teenage years where authority was no friend of hers. She was staying out late at night, letting friends come over when Holly and Greg were at work, knowing that was against the rules. Holly had witnessed, on more than one occasion, Paige ignoring Lucy while she tried to talk to her because she was on her phone or using the laptop.

When she went up to her bedroom, she found Greg already in bed, reading a new book she had picked up for him a few days ago. She went to the bathroom, brushed her teeth, and changed into an over-sized T-shirt before coming back out. "Can we talk for a few minutes?"

He set the book on his lap, using his hand as a bookmark. "Sure."

"Lucy came to me a little while ago, upset because she doesn't think Paige likes her anymore."

Greg nodded. "Is it because of her friends?"

Holly climbed into the bed next to him. "Yeah. I tried to explain that Paige is a teenager, but I don't think she understood what I was saying."

"I spoke to Paige last night. We talked about her staying out late, having friends over, the type of people she's friends with. Christ, some of them scare me. She seemed receptive to what I said but we'll see if she makes any changes."

She leaned over and kissed him on the cheek. "Thank you for talking to her. It was a long time ago, but I remember what it was like being her age, or around her age, and I know she'll give us trouble, especially having Monica as a parent. I'm just worried she'll set a bad example for Lucy."

"I want to cut her a little slack because of what you've told me about Monica. But she has to learn that living here means she has rules that she has to follow. She can't just come and go as she pleases and if she wants to see her friends, that's fine. But she needs to ask permission before she invites them over."

"Mmm. I like it when you play the tough dad." She draped on arm across his waist and pressed her lips to his.

"You do, huh?" He set his book on his nightstand and pulled her close. His heart wasn't in it, but he would take what she was offering.

# Chapter 9

## The Conversation

Monica handed Paige a stack of papers she printed out. She had the entire conversation typed out already. "It's simple. Once you get in her computer, you can log into this chat room. The username and password are right at the top. I typed the entire conversation, both your lines and mine. All you have to do is type in what I've already written."

They met at a park, not too far from Holly's house. A bench sat in the back, along the tree line, hidden from view of the street and blocked by the tennis courts. Monica wore a zipped sweater with a hood that she used to cover her head and block her face. Every time she came into town, she always felt the need to hide for fear of someone from her childhood recognizing her, or worse, mistaking her for Holly. It was midday so the park was empty save for the few owners taking their dogs for a stroll.

"What if someone catches me? I'm not supposed to be in her office. She doesn't allow anyone in there, not even Greg, unless she's with them. There are two places in the house that are off limits to everyone and that's her office and his office. I'll be in so much trouble if she finds me in there, especially if I'm on her computer. She only uses it for work." Paige found the park a few days after she started staying with her aunt and uncle. She walked over a few days a week, even when it was cold, because it was quiet and she liked sitting on the benches watching the ducks in the pond. She could watch them for hours, dipping under the water and seeing the water bead and roll down their backs along their feathers. "There's another computer in the family room that is open for everyone to use. Can't I use the one out there?"

"No. You can't. The whole idea is that it needs to be her computer. It has to look like she's trying to hide it."

Before Paige moved in with them, Monica gave her an overview of some of the stuff she expected her to do. Everything seemed simple enough until she got to the house. It was much harder than she expected to pull off some of the tasks given to her. She needed to come up with a plan, something to say, if Holly, Greg, or even Lucy caught her in the office. She sifted through the papers in her hand. "Oh, gross. I can't type this stuff, especially to you. This stuff is.... disgusting."

"Suck it up. All you have to do is type it out, word for word. I did the hard part by coming up with everything already."

"Yeah, that's part of the problem. This is so gross. I don't want to know that you thought all this up." She faked a shudder and her face scrunched.

"Just do it and stop arguing about it. I'm sick of having the same conversation. Find a way to get yourself into the office and type up what I wrote. It's not that hard." Monica was getting irritated at Paige pushing back every time she told her to do something. It was part of the plan and Paige knew that since the beginning. The plan wouldn't work without her. "I can't do this without you so whatever it is that's bothering you, figure it out." She stood and walked away, leaving Paige sitting on the bench by herself. She knew she would come through somehow, whether she wanted to or not.

# Chapter 10

## It's All Her Fault

"Holly. Come in here for a minute. I have something I think you need to explain to me." Greg was pacing around his office, waiting for her to make her appearance. He spent hours trying to figure out what to say to her, trying to understand whether he should be upset or angry. The email he received through his work account had thrown him off. He knew Holly had been under a fair amount of stress lately between Paige moving in and Monica having no contact with them. They had both tried to get Paige to give them information about where Monica could be or what she might be doing but she resisted each time and told them she hadn't spoken to her since she dumped her on their doorstep.

Holly appeared in the entryway to Greg's office with a quizzical look on her face. "What's the matter? Why are you yelling clear across the house?" It was unlike him to yell for any reason. Even when he was angry, his voice might be stern, but he still kept the volume low. The look on his face worried Holly. His eyes glistened in the office lights and his face was a deep red. She had only seen him look like this once and it was when he had gotten into a physical fight with his brother over his parents' will.

"I don't even know what to say. I guess it's best to just show you the email I received and let you do the talking. God, Holly. Am I really that bad? I mean, I thought we agreed to talk about this stuff? Be open with each other? We both knew we would have to make sacrifices to make this lifestyle work."

Holly stared at the printout he was holding out to her, but she didn't take it. She had never seen it before. "I don't know what this is. Is this part of a chat, a text message? What is it?" The printout showed a back-and-forth conversation, half of it showing a bubble with her face in it, the other half, another man who wasn't Greg. It was clear it wasn't the entire conversation but some parts that she could see were explicit. "Greg, honestly, I have no idea what this is. Where did it come from?"

Greg twisted his face in disgust. "Don't play dumb with me. You know damn well what this is. It has your picture, your name. The entire conversation takes place during times that I wasn't home." He slammed the paper onto his desk. "I just don't understand why, if you were so unhappy, you didn't just come to me. You know you can talk to me about anything."

Holly did know she could talk to him. She also would have gone to him to discuss it if she were unhappy. But she wasn't unhappy with their marriage. The only thing she was currently not happy about was having Paige living with them with no idea how long she would be there, not knowing if or when Monica was coming back. The pattern of forgetfulness she had been exhibiting over the past month was a cause of distress. She felt like she was losing her mind, like she had no control over her own life, and this current situation wasn't helping. "I don't even know what this chat room is."

"Well, let's go look at your computer and your phone and we'll see if you know what it is."

She couldn't believe what she was hearing. He didn't believe that she wasn't part of this. "Okay, let's put your mind at ease. You won't find anything."

They both left his office, Greg storming out and Holly moping behind him. Holly was angry that he didn't believe her but also upset he thought so little of her. At least she was confident he wouldn't find anything on her computer. They entered her office and she booted up her computer, the silence between the two of them was unbearable. Holly was hovering over her desk, waiting for the password screen to pop up. When it did, she entered it and Greg nudged her aside, sitting in her desk chair. He began rooting through her folders, opening every file within. Finding nothing, he opened the internet browser and pulled up her history. Holly gasped, feeling like she would pass out. Just a few weeks ago, without her knowledge, something or someone wiped her computer history clean and now, staring her in the face, glowing on the bright screen, were chat rooms showing right at the top. There were a lot of them. With a quick scroll, it showed she had been logging in to and chatting on these sites for weeks. "Greg? This...this is impossible. I did not do this."

Greg was already sending the history to her printer and he spun toward her as the printer whirred to life. "Holly, Stop. Just stop. What, do you think Lucy did this? You think our nine-year-old daughter hacked into your computer and started a chat like this?" He grabbed the papers from the printer and shoved them into her hand. Pushing past her, he stomped out of the office, slamming the door behind him. Holly let the papers fall to the floor, she dropped into her chair and began to sob. *Was she really losing her mind? Who was this she was supposedly talking to? Why did she not remember talking to anyone, logging in to any chat rooms, or even creating an account?* She needed to find an explanation for this and she needed to find it fast. She could feel her life turning upside down and she felt powerless to stop it. She dropped her head to her desk and then shot up to a straight sitting position. *Paige!*

She gathered the papers from the floor and stormed down the hall, straight to Paige's room, furious. It had to be Paige; it was the only thing that made sense. She was using her name and picture to talk to people online. It was disturbing to think a young teenager could be having such explicit conversations with someone she most likely had never met and Holly was determined to put a stop to it immediately. She slammed Paige's door open, ready to confront her niece, and was disappointed to find that she wasn't there. Of course, she wasn't there. Holly sighed. *Why would she expect anything different?* She turned and went in the opposite direction, towards Greg's office, and knocked on the door. Without waiting for a response, she opened the door and found him sitting at his desk, slouched in his office chair.

"I have nothing to say to you, Holly. Nothing that comes out of your mouth is going to make me feel any better about any of this."

"Paige." She let the name linger in the air, hoping Greg would come to the same conclusion she did. He stared at her for a moment and then turned away, sighing. "Greg, that must be it. There's no other explanation. Teenagers are curious. She probably thought by using my name, she wouldn't get in trouble for talking to someone online or using my computer without my permission. She probably didn't even realize we would be able to see what she was doing."

Greg's mouth hung open; his eyes rolled up to the ceiling. "Holly. Jesus. Really? You're going to blame a teenager for having conversations like this? That is the most ridiculous thing I've ever heard. This type of blame is low, even for you. She's a freakin' child. And right now, you're also acting like one. Just accept the fact that I caught you. It's really a very simple thing to do. You're a woman in your forties, it's time for you to take responsibility for your actions."

"But I. Didn't. Do this." She threw the papers in his direction and watched them flutter to the floor.

"Okay, Holly. Let's pretend for a moment that it was Paige. Why would the person she was chatting with feel the need to send them to me? How would he have my email? Hmm? These chats show that you met, in real life. I can only assume this man would be smart enough to figure out, when he saw her, that Paige is only a child and not a married woman." He spat the last words at her, causing her to take a step back from him. "I...I need time to think. Get out of my office."

# Chapter 11

## The Party

"Who invited your sister to this party?"

Holly rolled her eyes. "I have no idea. I don't think Shaun actually invited many people, just if you heard about it, you could come. She must have heard about it."

"She's not even talking to anyone." Music was pumping into every room, the bass making it feel like every beat was jolting their insides. "You should tell her to go home."

"I can't. She has every right to be here. I don't know why she would want to be, she's not friends with anyone here. Still, she's allowed." She took a sip from her cup and her upper lip curled. "Mike probably could have sprung for better beer."

Holly's friend, Janet, was best friends with Monica until eighth grade. During their freshman year, they didn't have any classes together, but

Holly and Janet did. Over the course of that year, the two pushed Monica to the side.

"I have an idea. I'll be right back."

A few minutes later, Holly watched as Monica walked out the back door with a guy she recognized from the halls around school. She locked eyes with her sister and Monica smirked as she slipped through the doorway with the guy's hand on her lower back.

Holly didn't give it a second thought when the same guy brushed by her about twenty minutes later, nor when she didn't see her sister the rest of the night. She poured herself into bed just after one o'clock. She always had obscure dreams when she had been drinking and tonight had been no exception. The spritz from the squirt gun felt so real on her face. Beads of water rolled over her chin and down her neck, cold like ice. Muffled voices sounded in the distance, someone called out her name. Another shot of water landed on her shoulder, a second directly next to her eye. Her name, closer this time, someone pushed her, tackled her, and slammed into the ground, pinned down by her shoulders. "How could you just leave me there?" A final drop of water landed on her forehead, jolting her awake. She struggled, twisting to ease the hold against her shoulders.

"Get off me."

"Not until you tell me why you left."

Holly managed to slide one leg from under her sister. She twisted her torso and pulled her leg up, catching Monica's hip with enough force to knock her off the bed. She caught sight of the clock on her nightstand telling her it was five in the morning. She pressed her fingers to her temples, already feeling the effects of too much alcohol. "Are you just getting home? Mom and Dad are going to kill you."

Monica stood, shaking, water dripping from the ends of her hair.

"Why are you wet?"

"Probably because my sister left me alone at that party and I had to walk home in the pouring rain after Shaun locked me in the shed out back. Did you even bother to look for me?" She crossed her arms over her chest, shivering.

Holly laughed, louder than she intended. "You got locked in a shed?"

"It's not funny. I had to bust out a window to get out. It was either that or go at the door with a hatchet."

She wasn't sure if it was the alcohol, exhaustion, or both but Holly had fallen into a state of giggles. "You broke a window on someone else's property and then walked home? In the rain? That party was like four miles away."

"You don't feel bad at all, do you?"

Holly's face grew serious and her giggles subsided. "Why should I? I didn't bring you to that party and you're not my responsibility."

"No, I'm not your responsibility, I'm your sister." Her words filled the room and Holly cringed back.

"Keep your voice down. And, yeah, I'm your sister but you make really stupid decisions. I can't watch you all the time."

# Chapter 12

## Medication Should Help

"I don't want to do this. An adult is one thing but she's only a child. Shit, I'm still a child. Is there really no other way?" Paige didn't mind helping Monica with the easy stuff, but this is different. Lucy is a little kid. She didn't want to be responsible for anything that may or may not happen to her. It wasn't fair for Monica to bring a young child into her troubled relationship with Holly.

"You have to do it, otherwise our entire plan will go to shit. This is what we planned, Paige. This is exactly what is supposed to happen. What was the point of doing all the other stuff we did if we aren't able to accomplish what we set out to do? Stop being such a baby, whining because you're afraid to hurt someone. What has Lucy ever done for you? What have any of them done for you besides feeling bad for you? What, they bought you new clothes? Clothes don't mean anything. You can walk around, wrapped in a sheet for all I care. Anyone who is worth anything won't care what kind of clothes you're wearing. People who matter will like you for you." She leaned against the counter with her arms crossed in front of her.

Paige put her head down in both shame and anger, waiting to see which would come out of her mouth first. "That's probably the first bit of parental advice you've ever given me and *that* means nothing coming from someone who's always immaculately dressed. I love these clothes. I love them because they fit and because they're new. Not just new to me, but actually new. I like the idea of being the first person to own them. I finally have shoes that fit my feet and for the first time ever I don't look like I crawled out of a dumpster. But they don't change who I am, they just make me feel better."

"Holly and Greg can give you anything you want but they don't do it because they love you. They probably don't even like you. I already told you they feel bad for you. They don't care about you, Paige, just like they don't care about me. It had been twenty years since I left and do you think Holly ever once tried to find me? No. Do you know why? It's because she thinks she's better than me, she thinks she's better than us. That's why we're doing this, to prove to her that she's not better."

"You keep blaming her for not ever trying to find you but you're the one who moved around constantly and you never tried to find her either. But I don't care what the reason is, they're nice to me. They treat me like I'm their own daughter. I get homecooked meals, I've even learned how to cook some things. Holly has taught me how to clean properly and I never feel like I'm in their way. I don't care if Holly buys these clothes for me just because she doesn't want to see me wearing rags anymore" She stopped to catch her breath and Monica waited for her to continue, letting her get it all out of her system. She likes showing off how much money she has and she cares about it a lot. Greg does, too, but he cares more that she spends so much of it. I heard them talking one night and he was mad that she was spending so much on me. He yelled at her because within a month of me living there, I went from having three outfits to a closet and dresser full. But I didn't ask her to buy the stuff. She volunteered the first time we went to the mall together and then she bought me a ton of stuff for Christmas. That's not my fault."

"You're right. It's not your fault. So why is Greg trying to blame you for what Holly's doing?"

Paige sat on the arm of the mustard-colored chair and felt it rock beneath her. It was coming unglued from the body and she liked to test it to see how long it would hold on. "He wasn't exactly blaming me. He just told her she was spending too much on me and that he noticed she wasn't buying Lucy as much."

"Did you tell him she's voluntarily buying you stuff? Or were you too scared because you didn't want him to know you were eavesdropping? This is the whole point in what we're trying to do here. You need to find time to tell him, let him know you overheard the conversation and then take it a step further and tell him you've asked her to stop buying you so much stuff. You have to say something."

"I'm not going to tell him that. The next time she buys me something, I'll make sure Greg can hear us, and I'll tell her I don't need all this stuff. Not because I don't appreciate it, I just don't need it. That will probably be enough for her." She turned and stretched so her feet were resting on the other arm of the chair and she heard the arm groan and splinter under her weight. "When I first moved in, I thought they were so loving toward each other, it's the first time I've ever been around a family like theirs. But then I realized they aren't that loving; they show each other love with material possessions. I also thought they were both really attentive to Lucy, but I was wrong about that too. They leave her alone most of the time, she plays in her room or watches television. Greg works really long hours and Lucy mostly sees him on weekends and they're usually running errands. I think I'm home more than he is and I've been staying out later and later trying to get them mad. But they act like it's just a normal thing for teenagers to do. Sometimes I don't think they even notice I'm gone."

Monica rolled her eyes. "Well, enough of that sob story." She reached into the refrigerator and pulled out a bottle of stand brand Cola. She drank half of it before settling on the middle cushion of the couch, pulling her legs beneath her. "Back to Lucy. Tonight, right?"

Paige had no idea what to do. She had done everything Monica had asked of her so far, but she didn't know if she could pull this off. She still had hours to go and she was already shaking and sweating just thinking about it. "I don't know if I can handle this. This isn't putting a piece of paper in a bag or typing something up. This is serious." Her voice sounded shaky and timid. "As much as I don't care for Lucy one way or the other, she's just a child. I don't understand how you can even consider doing this. Why would this even be a thought in your head? This is complete insanity."

"Oh, my God, Paige. You're killing me. After all the stuff you've done already, you really want to blow it now? Do you have any idea how much trouble I can get you in?" She stood and leaned over so her face was inches from Paige's. "You need to understand something, you don't have a choice. You signed up for this, remember? Who gives a shit about the kid? Stop over thinking everything. As a matter of fact, just stop thinking. Do what I tell you to do and get it over with." She straightened her body and crossed her arms again.

"I don't have time to pay with you. Every time I ask you to do something, you get all scared and don't think you can handle it. Suck it up because this is what life is like. It's not fair and it's not easy, but you manage to get through. Now take these, put two of them in her water before she goes to sleep and make sure she drinks it all and text me once everyone goes to sleep. Got it?" She dropped the pills in Paige's hand and opened the door for her. Paige walked down the front steps with her shoulders hunched. "Do not screw this up for me, Paige."

# Chapter 13

## It May Look Superficial but the Trauma Runs Deep

For the past two weeks, Paige had taken to putting Lucy to bed. She was trying to show Holly and Greg that she could be responsible and part of that was getting Lucy ready for bed and telling her a story or reading to her every night. It was Monica's suggestion and part of the preparation for tonight's plan. She had taken the long way home from her walk that afternoon, dreading stepping foot in the house. She knew she wouldn't be able to think of anything else for the next six hours. When she got back, she said 'hello' to everyone and immediately locked herself in her bedroom. She took the pills out of her pocket and rolled them around in her palm. Looking at them, she felt her heart rate quicken and her throat tighten as if she might throw up. She knew she had to do it, but she wasn't convinced she could. She didn't care much for Lucy, she found her to be annoying and clingy, but she still didn't want to hurt her. Monica had at least made this part a little easier on her by only requiring her to drop the pills in her water. Monica would take care of the rest.

Paige heard a gentle knock on her door and saw it begin to swing open. Startled, she shoved her fisted hand under her pillow and leaned down to make it look like she was resting. Her aunt poked her head in the door.

"Hey, I wanted to come check on you. You seemed a little distracted when you got home. Is everything all right?" She wore a look of genuine concern.

Paige clenched her teeth, still fighting the curdling feeling in her stomach and she forced a smile. "Oh, thanks for asking. I'm fine, just feeling a little under the weather. I think I'm just tired." Feeling like her position was giving away that she was hiding something, she loosened her fist, letting the pills fall from her hand, and moved so her elbow propped her up. "I think I'll read to Lucy and then head to bed myself. I'll probably feel better in the morning."

"Okay. Are you sure you want to put Lucy to bed? I can do it if you're not feeling well. You could just sleep now if you want."

"No, it's fine. I like putting her to bed. Besides, reading to her may help me relax a little bit, too. Giving you a little free time makes me feel like I'm contributing to the family." She put on her best smile, hoping Holly wouldn't see right through it. Paige really didn't care about being part of the family anymore, Monica's words had poisoned her against the attention she was getting. Now, she was simply biding her time until she could leave, she wanted to finish what she started so she could walk away from it all. After six months, she felt she was beginning to crack under the pressure and she wasn't sure how much longer she could keep up her performance. Leaving was the only thing keeping her motivated. From what she had done so far, she felt she deserved an Oscar.

"Okay, well, have a good night. And thank you for taking care of Lucy. She really does enjoy it when you read to her at night." Holly smiled and closed the door behind her.

Paige sat up and breathed in deeply. That was close. She had about an hour before she had to put Lucy to bed and she was hoping she could pull it off. She stood up, walked to her dresser, and turned the radio on. Listening to music often helped her relax, she just had to hope she didn't fall asleep while she was waiting. With every minute that passed, a new knot formed in her stomach and she was counting down until it was time to go get Lucy.

She dropped two pills in her pocket and crept down the stairs to the kitchen. Filling a glass with water, she looked over both shoulders before retrieving the tablets from her pockets. She dropped them in the water and watched as they dissolved, more rapidly than she would have thought. Once the last trace of them disappeared, she walked to the family room and found Lucy curled up on the sofa. "Ready for a story and bed, Lucy?" Her voice shook as the words came out. She needed to calm herself down. Her hands felt as if they were vibrating and she was beginning to sweat. At least if Holly ran into them, her story about not feeling well would hold up.

"Yup." Lucy hopped off the couch and hit the power button on the remote. She was already wearing her pajamas, pink fleece pants and a fleece buttoned top with My Little Ponies on them. Paige hated to admit it, but they looked so warm and comfortable. She thought she would appreciate them now, even at her age, since she never got a chance to enjoy them when she was small. Lucy skipped by her and slowed once she got to the stairs. It was the same every night. She would be full of energy until she hit the stairs and then she made a big production over how hard it was to physically climb them. Once she was in bed, the energy came back in full force and she flipped, kicked, thrashed, and moved all over the place until she could get comfortable. It usually took close to an hour to get her to calm down enough that she could listen to a story before falling asleep. Paige sighed as she realized that wouldn't be the case tonight. Tonight, she would calm down and, before Paige could finish the first scene of the book, would most likely fall asleep.

"Up the stairs, kiddo. No wasting time tonight." Her voice held zero conviction and Lucy continued to climb the stairs like a sloth. She took one step at a time, first with one foot then the other, as if she were a three-year-old learning to climb them. On any other day, this annoyed Paige, but tonight, the longer Lucy took to get up the stairs, the longer Paige could put off the inevitable.

Lucy sat on her bed and Paige handed her the water glass, shaking so hard she sloshed some onto the carpet. She felt as if her conscious was going to shatter into a million pieces. "Make sure you drink all of this. I'm not feeling very well and this water will help you not catch whatever it is that I have. I would feel awful if I got you sick." She leaned over and fluffed up Lucy's pillow while she drank the water. "Wo, what would you like tonight? Do you want me to tell you a story or read you a book?"

"Hmm. Book." She stayed sitting on the side of the bed, water glass in hand, kicking her feet up and down. She looked so innocent in her pink, fuzzy pajamas.

"Reading it is. Hurry up and drink your water so you can lay down." Paige turned to Lucy's bookcase so she could choose a book from the shelf. She took a few deep breaths and tried to remember what Monica had told her. *'It's not going to hurt her. All it's going to do is make her sleep a little deeper so she won't feel or remember anything. It's perfectly safe.'* Paige sighed and chose a book at random.

As Paige predicted, Lucy fell asleep almost as soon as she laid down. Paige stayed in her room a while longer and continued reading just in case Holly or Greg happened to walk by. She didn't think they would believe her if she told them Lucy fell asleep right away so she finished the entire book, pretending she was still entertaining her. As much as she believed it would cut down on any suspicion, she also stayed as a means of killing time until she had to text Monica. She read two complete books before standing, unlocking the window, and placing the books back on the shelf. She closed the door quietly behind her, unsure why she took so much care in doing so. Lucy wasn't waking up any time soon.

In the morning, sun streamed through Paige's window and it made her squint. Her head was pounding. The pain tempted her to pull a pillow over her head and stay in bed, not wanting to play the oh-no-what-happened game so she didn't bring any suspicion her way. Thinking better of it, she stretched and pulled on her slippers. She could hear Holly's voice as she descended the stairs and it gave her pause. She listened for a few moments and, determining that Holly's voice was calm, she continued. She noticed Holly was on the phone so she went to the refrigerator to pour herself a glass of orange juice.

Holly smiled at her while she finished her call. "Good morning. Are you feeling better?"

Paige shrugged her shoulders. "Quite a bit. I slept really well last night. I do have a bit of a headache, though." The fact was, she barely slept at all. She tossed and turned most of the night with a sort of nervous energy.

"There's aspirin in the cabinet above the sink if you need it." She was shuffling papers and stuffing them into her work bag as she spoke. "Hey, have you seen Lucy yet? It's pretty late for her to still be sleeping. She needs to get ready for school and I can't be late to work this morning."

Paige pinched her lips and shook her head. "I can right downstairs when I woke up."

"I'll go get her."

As Holly went up the stairs, Paige's grip on her juice glass tightened so much she feared it would shatter in her hand. She set it on the counter as she reminded herself over and over to stay calm. It wasn't that big of a deal.

"Oh my God. Lucy, what happened?" Holly screamed from upstairs.

Paige began to shake uncontrollably. She could hear murmurs of conversation from Lucy's bedroom and she wanted to run out the door, never to look back. She placed her hands over her nose and mouth, willing herself to calm down, bracing herself for what she was about to see. As soon as she heard them coming down the stairs, she picked her glass back up and leaned against the counter as casually as she could.

Lucy was screaming at her mother to put her down and she could tell Holly was wrestling her way to the kitchen. "Paige. Get an ice pack from the freezer. Wrap it in a dish towel."

She could hear the concern in Holly's voice and immediately moved to grab a towel. "Is everything okay?" She couldn't think of what else to say. She closed the freezer door and finally caught a glimpse of Lucy. Holly had a tight grip on her, but she was pushing against her, struggling to push her away. Paige gasped and threw her hand over her mouth. She thought she might be sick.

"I don't know what happened." She sat Lucy on a chair, catching a foot in her ribcage as she did so, and grabbed the ice pack from Paige. Pressing it against Lucy's face she turned toward Paige with a pained expression. The entire side of her face is swollen and her eye is swollen shut and bruised. It looks like someone punched her." Lucy was still struggling to put distance between herself and her mother. "I'm not sure what's happening, maybe it was a bad dream or something, but she's acting like she's afraid of me."

Against her better judgment, Paige stepped forward and put out her hand. "Here. Let me." She took the ice pack from Holly and moved to get a better look at Lucy's face. She felt her throat tighten again and she had to look away so she didn't lose her juice in Lucy's lap. A sweat broke out over her entire body and her head was swimming. "I think you need to call the doctor."

"Nooo." Lucy whined and pulled her face away from the cold pack, pouting. "I don't like the doctor."

"Honey, we need to make sure you're okay. Are you sure you don't remember anything from last night? Did you have a bad dream? Did you fall out of bed?" Holly tried to prompt her to give any information she had, but so far, she had had no luck.

Lucy recoiled at the sound of Holly's voice but didn't say a word.

Paige wanted to know, for her own emotional state, if Lucy remembered anything. "Lucy? Can you remember anything from last night? We're just trying to make you feel better."

She looked at her with her one good eye. "Uh-uh. I remember you getting a book. I think I fell asleep fast. Sorry." She looked down at the floor and winced.

"That's okay. You can sleep when you're tired. Do you remember anything else?" Paige was kneeling in front of her with a hand resting on one of Lucy's, trying to bring her some form of comfort.

"I remember Mommy coming in once and waking me up and then she came in again this morning and yelled at me and scared me."

"Honey, maybe you were dreaming. I fell asleep last night and slept through the whole night." Holly looked concerned, as she should be.

Her daughter was hurt and she had no idea how it happened. But Lucy kept insisting that she was in the room with her last night. It didn't make any sense. "Either way, we are going to take you to the doctor. Just for a checkup."

Lucy's mouth turned down and she slid off the chair, taking the ice pack from Paige. She held it against her face while she shuffled to the family room to watch television.

"Great," Holly grunted. "I'll have to take her out of school for the day and I need to call out of work. Boy, my boss is going to love this. Do you know how many times I've had to leave work for one reason or another recently? I think his patience is wearing thin with me." She grabbed her phone from the counter and headed toward her office.

Paige didn't reply but let out a long breath and closed her eyes. Holly was dealing with this much better than she expected. She went to the family room to sit with Lucy until it was time for her appointment.

Holly was dreading the phone call to Greg. She had already called Martin and told him she would have to work for home for the day and would be working a longer shift to cover the time for the doctor's appointment. She explained the situation without going into too much detail and, as expected, he wasn't happy but told her to take the day and they would talk about it when she got to work the next day. It wasn't a comfortable call, but it was easy compared to the one she would have to make to Greg. She called his phone and wasn't surprised he let it go to voicemail. He hadn't spoken a single word to her since they left the school the previous afternoon. She ended the call without leaving a message and brought up her text messages. She typed a quick message asking him to call her as soon as possible because it was important. She told him she needed to take Lucy to the doctor, hoping it would prompt him to call her back. It worked. As soon as the message showed on his phone he called her back.

"What's wrong with Lucy." There was no greeting, just the question.

"Hello to you, too. But I'm not really sure." She explained how she found Lucy when she went to wake her up and as much as she wanted to hide the information from him, she was honest and told him what Lucy had been saying about the previous night. She was concerned about the meeting at the school yesterday and worried people would believe one of them was actually hurting Lucy. She heard Greg grunt into the phone.

"Are you sure bringing her to the doctor is a good idea? After what happened at school yesterday, this is a worst-case scenario. DCS is already planning an unannounced visit to the house. We're already harboring a teenager who doesn't go to school, with no way of getting in touch with her mother. I still haven't figured out how we're supposed to explain her presence. And now, our child has a battered face, that supposedly happened while she slept, and she wants to blame you for it. DCS will surely show up on our doorstep in no time."

"And if we don't bring her in and we send her to school with a black eye and swollen face, we'll have DCS on our doorstep wondering how it happened and why we didn't seek medical treatment. It will look like we were trying to hide it." She sighed. "Her face looks bad, Greg. I really think we need to bring her in to have her looked at." She hated arguing with him and it was beginning to stress her out. At a time like this, she believed they should be banding together but he seemed focused on pushing them further apart.

"Do what you want. But if the police of DCS shows up at our house, you can deal with them yourself. I'm not getting involved in any of this. And why, exactly, is Lucy insisting that it was you who woke her up last night?"

That was it. Holly knew beyond all reason that he no longer trusted her. Not just in their personal relationship, but in life in general. As strong as she considered herself to be, she instantly broke down with the realization. Tears spilled down her cheeks and she croaked out, "I'll let you know what the doctor says." She ended the call and dropped the phone on her desk before crumbling to the floor. She never believed her life would come to this. They had worked too hard to make the life they both desperately wanted and it was all crashing down around her. There were too many situations over the past few weeks for her to believe they were all coincidence. She didn't know what the game was or who was playing it, but she wanted no part of it. She realized she would have to take matters into her own hands if she wanted answers. She stood and walked down the hall to her bedroom's en suite. She washed her face, gave her reflection a pep talk, and went back to her office to call the doctor.

# Chapter 14

## An Apple a Day

Holly practically had to carry Lucy to the car. She kicked and screamed the entire way out. She grabbed the side of the door and smashed it into Holly's arm, accidentally, when she tried to put her in the backseat. "I don't want to go with you."

Holly grunted and slammed the door closed. She heard Lucy scream from inside, "I want Paige."

She threw her purse in the passenger seat and pulled her phone from her pocket before climbing into the driver's seat. "You can see Paige when we get home."

The doctor agreed with Holly that it did look as though someone had physically assaulted Lucy, but also explained that she may have hit her face falling out of bed. "If she were dreaming when it happened, it's very possible that she wouldn't remember. It's rare but I have seen and heard of cases where a person dreams about something and wakes up with physical bruises or scratches from the event."

Holly cocked her head to the side, not fully believing what he told her.

"For example, someone may dream a house cat is attacking them. They'll wake up with scratches on their arm, but they don't own a cat. The scratches were self-inflicted while that person was dreaming."

"So, you think she fell out of bed and landed on her eye?"

"Not at all. Do you see this spot here? See how it's a much darker shade of purple than the surrounding area? That's probably where the impact was. She could have hit her face on something on the floor or hit a desk or nightstand on the way down. Our eyes are extremely sensitive and any trauma that happens near them can cause them to swell."

Hearing that made Holly feel much better, although she still wasn't sure she believed it. She asked if she could speak to him privately for a moment and they left Lucy in the room by herself while they stepped into the hall. She didn't want to make Lucy feel any worse than she already did. The patient rooms all had murals painted on the walls in fun, primary colors. The computer mice had mouse ears and a tail glued to them and the monitors all sported a pair of rabbit ears to make the children more comfortable. The hallways were untouched and they wore the same pea green paint on the walls that most hospital corridors had. They weren't welcoming at all.

Holly explained about the meeting at the school the previous day. "I was hesitant to bring her in today and Greg didn't want me to bring her in at all. He was concerned about people thinking we hurt Lucy and the last thing we want is someone from social services to show up at our door. Accident or not, this is the worst timing for something like this to happen. I argued and brought her in any way because of how bad it looks. I didn't want her to go unchecked in case there was something more serious going on."

The doctor recognized the look of concern on her face. No parent ever wants to see their child hurt or in pain. "Holly, I have known you and Greg for years. You're good parents and I can see how concerned you are about the situation. I can't say I wouldn't feel the same way if I was in this position. However, you can rest assured that no one from DCS or the school has contacted me. If there is a real concern, DCS usually reaches out immediately to request a child's medical records to see if they indicate any form of abuse or unusual and unexplained injuries. Lucy has never had anything like that and no one has contacted me about her. Before you leave, I'll write a note for you to bring to the school stating that we saw Lucy in the office today and they may contact me directly with any questions regarding her injury."

Holly forced Greg into the kitchen as soon as he got home from work. She was determined to have a conversation with him whether he was a willing participant or not. Since it concerned Lucy, she thought he might be willing. She joined him at the table and for the first time, got a good look at his face; he looked tired. She realized the situation was taking a toll on him, even his suit looked slack and not as crisp as it usually was.

Greg had yet to see Lucy because Holly grabbed his attention before he had a chance. "I wanted to warn you first before you see Lucy. I don't know what happened and the doctor couldn't say for sure either, but he did tell me she's fine aside from the bruising. He just wants her to take it easy for a few days. He also told me not to worry about DCS. He said if they do reach out to him, he doesn't have anything to show them to suggest that we've abused Lucy in any way. He's on our side. I think..."

Greg interrupted her, his voice stern and deeper than usual. "I think we need to talk about Paige."

"Paige? But..."

"No, Holly. We need to talk about this. Paige has been putting her to bed for weeks. She was the last one to see her last night. We need to think rationally about this." He slammed the side of his fist on the table.

Holly had no idea where the rage came from, but the words burst out of her mouth, louder than she had ever spoken to her husband. "Are you freakin' kidding me, right now? Why is it okay for you to blame Paige? I tried to have an open discussion with you about the possibility of her being the one on my computer and you wouldn't have any of it. You didn't even want to hear her name. Now, because it suits your theory, you're willing to blame her? That's not fair, Greg. That's not fair at all." Holly walked past his chair and stormed out of the kitchen. "Unbelievable!" She screamed back. She walked into the family room and back into the kitchen. "You know, despite everything, right now, the two of us need to stick together to figure out what's going on. You can be as mad as you want at me, but we can't go around blaming people for stuff because it seems like the easiest solution. We have bigger things to worry about here than trying to blame a child for something like this." Tears filled her eyes and spilled down her cheeks. She hated herself for being so emotional. She couldn't understand how things had gone so wrong in such a short amount of time.

# Chapter 15

## There's No Place Like Not Having a Home

Paige had made her way to the next town before sending a message to Monica. While she waited to hear back, she moved further away from Greg and Holly's house. The message she sent simply told Monica she needed to see her but didn't include the reason why. Rain began to fall over her, a drop here and there at first and became steadier as she continued. She was getting cold, the water seeping through her clothes. Before she left, she didn't take the weather into consideration. She focused her efforts on getting away. Over the last two years, she had forgotten what it was like to be outside, at the mercy of mother nature, with no options for getting away from the cold, rain, or wind. It took Monica two hours to respond to her message. She didn't ask where she was or what she was doing. She told her they would meet the next day and that was it. Paige turned off her phone to save the battery for Monica's incoming message the next day. She wondered if Monica knew she had left Greg and Holly's. She assumed the police hadn't made their way to her house yet.

In the distance, she could see an old barn behind a farmhouse. It would be a good place to shelter for the night. She hung around the area for most of the evening, watching for activity in the house and the barn, thankful the rain had finally stopped. The house had recently gotten a face-lift with a coat of fresh paint and a new front porch. Aside from the chicken coop on the side, it looked as if no one had thought about the barn in years. A dusting of feathers lined the ground, matted down by the rain and splotches of white feces clung to the boards and wire. It wouldn't be the worst place she had ever slept.

After the last light in the house went out, Paige carefully made her way through the backyard and into the barn. She was right about it looking abandoned, but there was a pile of hay she would be able to sleep on. It wasn't the most comfortable solution, as she knew from experience, but it would be warmer than sleeping on the ground. Walking all day exhausted Paige and she fell asleep almost instantly once she unknotted her blanket from her backpack.

The sound of the barn door scratching open early the following morning caused Paige to be rudely awakened. She had trouble seeing while her eyes were adjusting to the sunlight streaming through. Straining her eyes to see where she could hide, she heard someone shout.

"See that? I told you I heard the barn door open last night."

Paige had no way to escape unless she left her blanket behind, grabbed her backpack, and ran straight through the two people who were standing in the doorway. "I'm sorry, I didn't mean to..." Paige choked out the words. She was scared. After all the time she had spent on her own, no one had ever caught her before.

"It's okay." The woman's voice sounded young. "Are you hurt in any way?"

Paige shook her head then realized they may not be able to fully see her, either. "No, I'm all right. I...I just wanted a place to sleep, out of the rain. I'll leave now." She bent to retrieve her blanket and bag.

"Nonsense. Come on inside, you can warm up a bit and I'll cook you some breakfast." She turned to go back to the house. Sensing Paige's reluctance, she turned back again. "Don't worry. You're not in any type of trouble, I just can't, in good conscious, allow you to leave without getting anything to eat. After breakfast, you can go on your way without any consequences." She motioned for Paige to follow her to the house.

Once inside, Paige could feel her body begin to thaw. The woman offered her a cup of coffee which she gladly accepted, wrapping both hands around it.

"Eggs and bacon, okay?"

"Uh, yes. That's more than enough." Paige looked at her, trying to place the voice with her face. The woman was much older than she sounded. "You really don't need to go through all this trouble, I'll just…"

"It's no trouble, I make us breakfast every day. Ted used to enjoy a big breakfast before he went to work and since we've retired, I've continued doing it. I'm Pam, by the way. What's your name?"

"P-Lucy." She immediately regretted the name choice, believing she might as well have told her her real name.

"Well, it's nice to meet you, Lucy. You know, it's funny, and I mean no offense to you, but I'm glad we found you this morning. I told Ted last night I heard the barn door open and he told me I was acting crazy. He refused to go out to look to see if anyone was out there. At least now he knows I was telling the truth." Seeing the look on Paige's face, she knew she didn't care about the story she was telling. She switched tactics to try to get her to talk. "So, Lucy, are you from around here or are you just passing through?" It didn't sound right when it came out of her mouth, the girl had spent the night in their barn. She promised her she wouldn't call the police; she was just curious what such a young girl was doing traveling on her own.

Paige looked at her with a mix of confusion and disgust. "I'm just passing through. I have an aunt that lives a few towns over so I'm going to stay with her for a while." It sounded as good as any other excuse she could think of.

"Oh, that's nice. I used to stay with my aunt during the summers when I was growing up. Oh, if only I could go back and have just one more summer with her." She sighed and her face fell. "Is there anything I can help you with? I can give you a ride, if you'd like, so you don't have to walk."

"No, thank you. I actually like walking. Besides, as long as it doesn't rain again tonight, I should be fine."

Paige finished her breakfast, helped Pam clear the table, and set off. She knew it was too early to hear from Monica, but she turned her phone on and took a route that went in the opposite direction she needed to go. If Pam chose to call anyone, she wanted her to point them in the wrong direction. Paige didn't want anything to do with the police and she definitely didn't want them to follow her to Monica's.

# Chapter 16

## Lunch Break

Holly had no idea what to do. Everything that was going wrong, she wanted to blame Paige, but she couldn't find a feasible explanation for why she would do any of it. Her and Greg still weren't talking and she desperately needed someone to talk to, someone without a biased opinion. She called her friend Janet to see if they could meet for lunch.

When they arrived at the cafe, they found a corner table hidden in the back. Normally, Holly would choose one close to the entrance, but she didn't want anyone to hear their conversation. She was having a hard enough time trying to process everything that was happening and the last thing she wanted was someone at the next table over thinking she was a lunatic who forgot to take her medication. The cafe was a regular place for them to meet, situated half-way between their workplaces. It needed an upgrade, but Holly found the older appearance soothing. She waited until they had their drinks and had placed their sandwich order before diving into the reason she asked Janet to meet her. They were still close friends but sometimes went six months without seeing each other.

Holly gave her a brief introduction to the fact that Paige had been living with them and then started with the simplest of strange occurrences, hoping Janet would have an easy, rational explanation. She told her about the permission slip for Lucy's zoo trip and then moved on to the email that disappeared. She gave her all the details about never deleting her history, saving the file itself, having a lock on her laptop.

Janet stared and nodded her head while she listened to Holly. "Well, who can we eliminate from the suspect pool?"

"Lucy, to start with. She's way too young and wouldn't know how to cover her tracks." She thought about Greg and Paige and which of the two was least likely to be guilty.

"So, we're left with either Paige or Greg, right?"

"Yeah, but neither of them knows my password. And I don't think Paige knows enough about computers to be able to hack into one." She took a long sip of iced tea and stared at the ceiling. "So, let's pretend it was Greg. Why would he do that?" Holly grew angry thinking he may be the one behind that. "What would he have to gain by getting me in trouble with my boss?"

"Maybe he wants you home more?"

"Greg is gone more than I am. He leaves before me in the morning and comes home much later most evenings. As it is, I have dinner ready for all three of them at night and I take care of Lucy and Paige. Besides, wouldn't it be easier for him to just tell me he wants me home more? We had an open, communicative relationship before all this started to happen." She stopped speaking when the server brought their sandwiches over. She hadn't yet told Janet about the explicit chat Greg saw or Lucy's black eye.

"Should he come right out and tell you? Yes, of course. But that doesn't mean he will. Maybe he's worried about Paige being there by herself? You said yourself that her moods were beginning to fluctuate."

"He should still discuss it with me. Trying to get me in trouble at work or potentially fired isn't really the best option, you know? He could ask me to take a leave of absence or something if he's that worried." She took another sip of her tea, having yet to touch her food. "There is more to the story though, a few things I haven't told you about yet. I couldn't bring myself to say them aloud."

They continued to talk while they ate their lunch. Janet didn't know what to say about Lucy, but Holly knew how direct Janet could be and had already mentally prepared herself for the question about the chat room.

"Were you talking to someone?"

"No, of course not. Until he showed me the email he received, everything was perfectly fine between us. Even with Paige being there, our relationship was just as good as it always has been. I think that's one of the reasons I'm so upset about it. If we had been fighting or growing apart or something, I could understand why he might think I would do something like that. But we hadn't been fighting and he still believed some random email over me." She dropped the rest of her sandwich and the plate clanked against the table.

"But it wasn't random, Holly. And you have to remember, you had a rough time a few years back. I can't tell you I wouldn't act the same way if I were in his position. You made some outrageous claims during that time. Maybe that's what he thinks is happening again. Have you been seeing your therapist?"

Holly nodded. "I have an appointment tomorrow. Can you explain to me how you don't think the email sent to Greg was random?"

"He could see it on your computer. It may not have been you that was doing it, but the fact is, someone was on your computer chatting with that guy. If..." She rolled her eyes to the ceiling as if deep in thought and then lowered her gaze to Holly again. "If that someone is actually a guy."

Holly's brow creased. "I don't know what you mean." She shifted in her chair, suddenly uncomfortable in her own skin.

"I mean, Greg was assuming it was you because it's your computer. Maybe we're all assuming it was a man because he stated that as a fact. None of us have ever seen him and people do stuff like that on the internet all the time. They send pictures that aren't of them, claim a job as their profession when they do something completely different, take on the persona of a different, real-life person. Do you mind me asking how long Paige has been staying with you?" Her eyes narrowed while she asked the question.

"I don't think Paige would do this. I thought so at first. I was convinced it had to be her. But she's only a child. There's no way she could have come up with this stuff on her own. I know she's had a tough life so far but..." Fear crept into her voice as she said the last word.

"Monica," the two women said in unison.

# Chapter 17

## The Walk

As soon as Holly got in her car, she sent Greg a text telling him she needed to speak to him as soon as possible and that she wanted to talk face to face. She told him it was important and ended the sentence with three exclamation marks. She threw her phone on the passenger's seat and sped out of the parking lot. Lucy had stayed home from school for the third day so she could rest and Holly had taken a few days off to stay with her. While she went out to lunch, she left Lucy at home with Paige. Once the realization hit that Monica may be the one behind everything, she threw a few dollars on the table to cover her tab and ran out the door. She didn't want Lucy spending time alone with Paige until she knew for sure what was going on.

Her tires squealed at the end of her driveway. She threw the car in park and jumped out before she had turned off the ignition. She sprinted to the door, tripping over a stone on the cobble walkway which accelerated her heart rate more than it already was. "Lucy," she yelled, flinging open the front door and running through the house. "Lucy? Paige? Where are you two?" She fled through every room on the lower level of the house. "Lucy," she called up the stairs. She took two steps at a time and threw open every door on the second floor, calling both girls' names. She ran back down the stairs and out the back door to check the yard. Her body dripped with sweat, her ears rang, her head felt like someone stuffed it with cotton.

Seeing the yard empty, she ran back through the kitchen and called 9-1-1 to report her daughter missing. The operator assured her they were sending a car over and she hung up and immediately called Greg.

He answered the phone with a huff. "I already sent you a message back." No greeting, no kind words.

"I don't care. I left my phone in the car. I left Lucy here with Paige and I got home and they're not here. I already called the police. They're..."

"The police? Holly, what in the world is wrong with you? You can't call the police. Did you forget..."

"Greg?" She yelled into the phone for the third time to get his attention. "I think it's Monica."

"Monica? Oh, Holly. What could she possibly have to do with this?" Instead of the concern from a moment before, annoyance had taken over in his voice.

"I think Monica is using Paige to get to us."

It finally dawned on him what she was trying to say. "I'll be right home." He ended the call and ran out of his office.

Two officers sat at the kitchen table when Greg rushed in, panting from running through the house. "Did you find her?"

Holly shook her head. "Not yet. I'm giving these officers all her information now. I still need to get her picture."

"I'll get one." He turned to go to the family room and almost ran straight into Paige and Lucy. "Lucy," he cried, dropping to his knees to give her a hug.

"Hi, Daddy. Why are the police here?"

Holly dropped down beside Greg and pulled Lucy toward her. "Oh, Lucy, we were so worried." She glared up at Paige. "Where the hell were you?"

Paige pulled back. "We went for a walk. I didn't think we were gone that long." She let her mouth hang open, unsure of what else to say.

"We went on a scavenger hunt." Lucy squealed with excitement about their adventure. "We had to find a rock and a stick and..." She ticked the items off on her fingers as she went through the list.

"Lucy, honey, why don't you go up to your room for a little bit and play before dinner. Daddy and I need to talk to Paige for a minute."

"Okay." Lucy put two hands on the stairs and hopped all the way up.

Holly glared at Paige again. "Kitchen. Now." She pointed to the two officers that had stood to leave.

Paige brushed past Holly, grabbed a bottle of water from the refrigerator, and sat at the table. "I'm really sorry, Aunt Holly. I didn't think it was that big of a deal. We were looking for something to do and it's so nice outside."

"You stay here for a minute. Greg, I need to speak to you." She walked the officers to the door and thanked them for coming out so quickly. As an afterthought, she also apologized for the false alarm. In truth, she felt stupid for not considering that the girls may have gone for a walk. She used to do it every day when she was young and Paige was right, the weather was beautiful. She should be thankful they were outside, enjoying nature. She led Greg upstairs to his office.

"You called the cops for that?" His eyes narrowed and he crossed his arms.

"Listen. I know you're mad about the police; I get it."

"No, you don't get it. Paige is staying here and there is nothing legal about it. We are not her guardians, she's still a minor, and we don't even have a way to get a hold of her mother. The police have no idea what's going on with the bruise on Lucy's face and I watched them both staring at her when she turned to go up the stairs. Nothing good is going to come from this, Holly."

"You need to hear me out. I think Monica is behind everything that's been going on lately. And I no longer believe Paige is her daughter."

"Have you completely lost your mind? "Greg rubbed his hands up and down his face. "What has gotten into you?"

"I went out to have lunch today and I was trying to find a rational explanation for what's been happening lately. All these things started when Paige moved in. She was here just long enough to get comfortable before everything started going to shit. And it makes much more sense if you consider that she may not be Monica's daughter."

"So, she made a mistake, which wasn't even a mistake, and all of a sudden you're not going to claim her as your niece anymore."

Greg spoke to her like she was an idiot. As he had so many times lately, she couldn't believe he was treating her like this. Except for a painful two years, they had always worked so well together, acted as a team. She had never seen this side of him and she didn't like it. She was beginning to think it may be a blessing in disguise. "Don't speak to me like that. You know damn well

I don't won't just throw her away like that. The other day, she was helping me wash the dishes and talked about what we were going to do over the next few months. When Paige was talking, she slipped and casually called Monica by her name. It came out as natural as could be, like she had been calling her that for years. Every time we talked to her about Monica, she always referred to her as 'my mother,' never 'my mom,' or even just 'mom.' Why would she have changed that? And why would it have come out so smoothly? I think something is going on that involves Monica and I am going to do everything I can to find out what it is.

"The first thing I'm going to do is talk to Paige to find out what really happened today. Then, I'm going to ask her about everything that has happened straight out. If, at that point, she doesn't admit any fault, then I'm going to follow her everywhere she goes for the next few days. I will get to the bottom of this. I will not stand by and let my so-called sister ruin our family. And I would appreciate it if you would come downstairs with me right now to speak to her about this." She turned her back on her husband and walked down the stairs.

She found Paige sitting at the table in the exact same position she was in when they left. She looked so innocent, so young. Looking into her eyes, Holly thought she must be wrong; there was no way a child could be a part of this. She thought about Monica and knew she needed to question Paige like she was an adult.

She grabbed a bottle of water and leaned against the counter, taking a few sips. In her head, she kept telling herself she needed to be stern, but at the same time she needed to remember that Paige was a child. Even if she could pull these things off, it was because Monica had given her the instructions to do so. She remembered well how vindictive and downright evil Monica could be when she put her mind to it. Now that she was thinking about it, if Paige were anything like Monica, maybe she could be capable of this sort of thing, even at her age. "Paige, we need to talk."

# Chapter 18

## Two Plus Two Doesn't Equal Four

Monica always had a difficult side to her. While the girls were growing up, people often referred to Monica as the 'evil twin.' She found trouble wherever she went and never stood up for herself to say why she did what she did, or in many cases, to tell people it wasn't her. Each time someone accused Monica of something she didn't do, she would do something else in revenge. She would steal Holly's dolls, write on them, black out their eyes with a permanent marker. She ripped the heads from their bodies and left them on Holly's pillow like a cat presenting its master with a gift by leaving a dead bird on the doorstep. The morning of their thirteenth birthday, Monica sneaked into Holly's bedroom and chopped a chunk of her hair off. Because she chose a piece in the front, Holly had no choice but to cut all her hair and she cried about it for three months while it grew enough so she no longer looked like a boy.

All the memories of what Monica had done raced through Holly's head. She realized, looking back, that a girl as young as Paige could do such things and because of her memories, also found her tactic for how to approach her. Just as she was sitting at the table, Greg appeared in the doorway, mumbled, 'sorry,' and took a seat.

"Paige, I want to apologize to you for being short with you earlier. I was upset when I came home and didn't find Lucy. I was worried, and as a parent, when you worry, panic mode sets in and sometimes it makes you irrational. I called the police because I had convinced myself in a matter of seconds that Lucy was in danger. I want you to know I'm not mad at you, I was just scared." She could feel Greg staring at her in disbelief and when she turned her head, he had his face scrunched in a way that said, "what the hell are you doing?" She turned back to Paige. "You know, when I see you and Lucy together it makes me so happy because I see sisters, not cousins. But that also makes me afraid because of how your mom and I were when we were growing up. Has she ever told you anything about our relationship?"

Paige stared at the table and shook her head 'no.' She was uncomfortable with Holly asking questions about Monica and she didn't want to be in a situation that would force her to answer questions about her.

"Well, I want to tell you a little about us so you know why I feel the way I do. It might help you understand. I wasn't always the nicest to her either, I'll take responsibility for that. Most of the stuff that happened wasn't harmful physically, but it was emotionally traumatizing. She made me mad one day, so I slashed her bike tires. Three days later, the day we turned thirteen, Monica sneaked into my bedroom while I was sleeping and cut a huge chunk of my hair off, right in the front. To fix it, I had to practically shave my entire head. I cried for months, every time I looked in the mirror, because I thought I looked like a boy. She used to follow me around on dates, just to make me uncomfortable. She would lurk in the shadows, waiting for an opportunity to embarrass me somehow."

Paige looked at her now, wondering where she was going with these stories.

"Our junior year, we had a fifteen-page paper due for our final exam. I spent two months writing mine while your mom was out every day, hanging out with friends. She kept saying she would get around to writing it. And she did. The day before it was due, she spent four hours at her computer, typing away. She printed it and left it on the counter so our mom could see it. I still feel bad because it's the worst thing I've ever done but I picked up her paper and started reading it, thinking it would give me a reason to make fun of her; she was never great in school. She wrote that paper so well, I couldn't believe it. It put my months' worth of work to shame. I couldn't let her turn it in."

"What did you do?" Paige was interested in the story now.

"I tore it up and threw it in the trash." Holly sighed, not wanting to admit the next part. "And then I deleted the entire thing from her computer. She got a zero for the assignment."

Greg grunted. "Why would you do that?"

"Because it was amazing. It doesn't make any sense now, as an adult, but when we were teenagers, it was the only thing I could think of doing. I was supposed to be the smart one, the one that always excelled in school. There was no way I could let her get a better grade on that than me." She gave Paige a look that asked if she was understanding everything before she continued. "I expected her to retaliate somehow, get revenge because she knew it was me, but she never did anything. She didn't even seem upset that all her hard work was for nothing. Months went by and she didn't bother at all. Until two days before we went to get our senior portraits taken. She started an argument with me, reminded me that I had destroyed her paper, and then punched me, as hard as she could, in the face. Even with tons of makeup on, I had a huge black eye in my portrait. I was the valedictorian of our class and everyone used that picture, including the local newspaper. It was humiliating."

"Holly, what does this have to do with anything? All these things happened years ago." There was a tone of frustration in his voice.

Holly sighed and looked at Paige. "Do any of these things sound familiar to you?" The point she was trying to make was that everything that was happening now had already happened on some level, years ago. She hoped Paige, or Greg, would see the connection.

Paige stared at her with a blank look on her face. "I already told you, Aunt Holly, my mom never talked about you. The day she dropped me off was the first time I found out you existed and all she told me was that you two didn't get along and she warned me that you might not be very happy to see her. I tried to ask her why she never mentioned you and she told me it was none of my business. She instructed me to stay out of trouble and then she left." Tears were beginning to fill her eyes and she wiped at them with the backs of her hands.

"Does it seem strange to you that everything that's been happening lately is the same type of thing that happened before?" She took a deep breath and looked at Greg, wanting to make sure he understood where she was going with this. He nodded and she continued. "Paige, do you know anything at all about what's been happening? Did your mom ask you to help her with any of this stuff? If she did, I want you to know you're not in any trouble. I just want to understand what's going on."

Paige stayed silent and stared at Holly. She took a quick glance at Greg, hoping he might help her, and then looked at Holly again. She had her hands folded on the table, her thumbs twiddling. Holly took that as a sign that she knew something but wouldn't say it. She wanted to stand up, grab Paige, and force the words out of her. She willed herself to stay calm even as waves of anger overtook her body.

"I don't know anything. I've told you that so many times already." Her voice was shaking and tears showed in her eyes again.

"All right," Greg finally chimed in. "I think that's enough for tonight. I understand you're upset but it's obvious she doesn't know anything. Paige, why don't you go up to your room for a while."

Holly huffed and Paige all but ran out of the kitchen. Greg and Holly sat in silence for a few moments, waiting to hear Paige's door slam upstairs. "Holly?" Greg sighed and leaned against the back of his chair, running his fingers through his hair. "I'm not sure what to say. You've told me before about some of the things from your past, but I didn't remember specifics, not even to put two and two together. Why didn't you tell me how much of a coincidence these things were? I know you're angry and we haven't been talking much but you should have said something."

For the first time in weeks, she saw compassion and love in his eyes. She thought he had finally come to his senses and believed what she was saying. "I tried to tell you, but you wouldn't believe anything that came out of my mouth. Aside from Lucy getting hurt, not having you believe me has been the hardest part. I know it was hard for you because of my past, when we lost Lauren, but right now, all I need is support, and I need it from you. You're the one who is supposed to listen to me, believe me, and be by my side no matter what." She ran her hands over her face, an involuntary gesture she made when she felt stressed. "I had lunch with Janet the other day. I had to talk to someone. The hardest part was having to tell her that we don't have the perfect marriage everyone thinks we do. I had to tell her that out of everyone in my life, you didn't believe me. And do you know what she did?"

Greg rolled his eyes and shook his head.

"She took your side. She said, based on my past, she would have done the exact same thing. Hearing that really hurt but after thinking about it for a while, I understood. I'm still not happy about it but I don't blame you, just like I don't blame Paige if Monica trapped her in the middle of this. But these things are too much of a coincidence. I am willing to admit it's possible that I've done some of these things without remembering but it doesn't feel the same as it did years ago. I don't believe it was me."

He looked surprised at her admission, but agreed with her. "I think we need to concentrate on Monica. Even if it's Paige doing these things, or helping her in some way, I don't think we should blame her. But you brought up a very good point a few weeks ago when you asked if Paige was really her daughter. What if she isn't? How did they meet and why are they so loyal to each other? How would a teenager get herself mixed up with your sister?"

Holly stood and walked to Greg, leaning over so she could hug him. "You have no idea how much it means to me that you're willing to listen." She sat back down and took a sip of her tea. "I think you're right. We should see if we can find out for sure whether they're actually related. Even though I haven't seen her in a long time, it wouldn't surprise me if Monica were running from something. We should find out where she lives. The fact that she thought to bring Paige here has to mean she lives close by, right?"

"Last I knew she was living in Florida in a rented trailer." Greg's voice trailed off when he realized what he was saying. His forehead broke out in a cold sweat.

"She what?" The last word echoed across the house as Holly slammed her fist on the table. Rage rose through her body. Her skin prickled with heat. "Say that one more time."

Greg lowered his head and his body sunk into itself. This piece of information had eaten away at him for years. He thought it would be better if Holly didn't know. "A number of years ago, before we lost Lauren, I found out where Monica lived. I went to see her, to ask her if she would be willing to reunite with you. But she shot me down. She told me she didn't want anything to do with you. I didn't tell you because I thought if you didn't know, you couldn't be upset about it. But I tried, Holly, I know how much she means to you, despite your history."

"Wait, wait, wait. You knew that Paige existed all this time and you didn't tell me?"

"No, that's just it. I had more than one conversation with her when we met. I even tried to convince her to come see you by showing her a picture of Lauren and she never mentioned having a daughter. Maybe she thought, if you knew, you would try even harder to get her back into your life."

She only heard half of what he said. Her mind focused on the fact that he found Monica and never told her. "So, you don't think she's her daughter?"

"I honestly don't know what to think. But I do find it odd that of all things, this is one she would choose not to mention."

# Chapter 19

## Plans Fell Through

Paige was thankful for Greg's interruption. She could feel her determination dwindling and she was afraid she would break down at any moment. Monica warned her months ago that Holly would question her about some of the stuff that was happening, but she didn't tell her there would be a full-on interrogation. As she was listening to Holly compare what happened during their teenage years to what was happening now, she started to get nervous. Holly was beginning to realize it wasn't her imagination. She knew Paige was behind these strange occurrences and now she was starting to think Monica was too.

Once Greg told her she could go, she sat at the top of the stairs, listening to their conversation. Monica's orders were to gather as much information as she could. She spent a lot of time sitting on the top step, eavesdropping on their private conversations. At first, she felt bad about the things she was doing. After hearing about all the stuff she did to Monica when they were younger, she didn't feel as bad. She thought Monica was just trying to ruin Holly's life, make her think she was going crazy again. She never told her about anything that happened in their past.

Paige had been keeping Monica up to date about anything she heard or saw that she thought might be significant or useful. Monica told her the information would be helpful in case they needed to change their course of action. The problem she faced was missing the end of conversations because she was afraid of someone catching her. The last thing she wanted to do was tell Monica they caught her eavesdropping.

Feeling their conversation coming to an end, she stood and moved to her bedroom. She laid in bed for hours questioning everything. Why was she so loyal to Monica? What was she doing to these people she barely knew, people she liked? Since moving into their house, she realized it was the most stable environment she had ever lived in. She liked where she was living; it felt good to feel loved. Living with Monica was like living with her own foster mother, the only exception was Monica took her off the street that her mother tossed her out on. *Was that why she was so loyal? Because Monica willingly gave her a bed to sleep in and a roof over her head?* She laid her head on her pillow and began to cry. She didn't want to have to keep doing this, but if she stopped, she wouldn't have anywhere to go again. And she couldn't blame Monica for everything, she agreed to what she was doing. She cried herself to sleep, trying to convince herself that this was worth it.

She awoke in the morning, reeling from a dream she had that caused memories to bubble to the surface of her consciousness. She remembered her bedroom growing up, mostly bare aside from a bed and a plastic storage shelf. Fluffy stuffed animals, beautiful dolls, and games filled her friends' rooms. Paige had only one doll that was losing its hair and had pen ink scratched across its cheek. Her deck of cards was missing a jack and an ace. For Christmas one year she received a teddy bear that was missing an ear, its fur crusted with an unknown substance, and a button eye that hung limply from its thread, exposing the pressure formed socket. She always wanted the same things her friends had until her mother kicked her out for the first time. She learned over the years to appreciate necessities over material possessions. The room she had at Monica's wasn't different from the one she spent years in. It was nothing more than a bed with threadbare sheets and a flat pillow that she had to fold in two.

Living with Monica felt different. She couldn't explain why but she felt she belonged there, like the two of them had a connection she never had with anyone else. Monica didn't have much to offer but she took Paige under her wing, gave her a roof, a bed, and food. At the beginning, they stayed out of each other's way. It wasn't until a month after she moved in that Monica told her why she was so willing to let a stranger stay under her roof and they spent the next two months going over the expectations Monica had for her. So far, she had done everything Monica asked and covered her tracks the best she could, but it wasn't good enough. Greg and Monica were starting to suspect her and she knew she had limited time left at their house. She crawled out of bed, hoping Monica would meet her early.

# Chapter 20

## He Came, He Saw, He Crumbled Under the Pressure

Eight years into their marriage, Greg felt as if he already knew Monica, even though they had never met. Holly talked about her every chance she got and it was clear to him, despite them not getting along, she loved her sister and would give anything to have a relationship with her again. For the first few years, he didn't give much thought to it, believing Monica would initiate contact if she had any interest in doing so. As time went by, he could see the toll her absence was taking on Holly and he made it his personal mission to try and find Monica. Maybe he would be able to convince her to give their relationship a try again.

It took him months to locate her. He tried utilizing social media first, spending hours scouring every profile with her name, looking for anything that connected one of them to Holly's hometown or any resemblance in facial features on profile pictures. He switched to paid online searches, those promising to find anyone, anywhere and quickly realizing they could, if said person didn't actively try to hide. Feeling defeated and out of options, he resorted to hiring a private investigator, looking for nothing more than a current address. It took the man three weeks. Greg paid him five hundred dollars in cash up front and met him only one more time, exchanging another one thousand for a folded piece of paper with a handwritten address on it. Two weeks later he boarded a plane to Florida with no plan other than to knock on Monica's door and hope for the best.

The address took him to a mobile home park that showed no signs of life. He parked his rented Mercedes in a dirt pull-off just outside the park and pocketed his keys after the third time verifying he had locked the car. The sign indicating that he was entering "Walter's Mobile Home Park" had become victim to the area's severe weather, crudely hanging from the one remaining screweye, the blue paint beaten to a dull hue. The air hung heavy with humidity and the fetid stench of the nearby swamp. He tried to breathe through his mouth, but it did nothing to relieve the tightness he felt in his throat, threatening to expel his late afternoon lunch.

Crabgrass crunched under his shoes as he tried to decipher the layout of the park. The layout of the homes was haphazard, with no discernable pattern. In the dying light of the day, his eyes scanned upended garbage bins, old, yellowing air conditioning units, a sagging mattress with circular stains the colors of dried blood and pea soup. Almost every home looked to come with a rusted-out Oldsmobile or small pickup, no longer capable of performing its intended duties.

Greg sighed, feeling lost in the maze of boarded up windows and rusted metal when he finally spotted the home he had been searching for. He paused to catch his breath, wondering why he hadn't thought to change out of his suit and tie. Sweat dripped down the side of his face, his sleeves and pant legs clung to his skin. He was only thankful for the long sleeves protecting him from the fog of mosquitoes that had been following him since he stepped out of his car.

Having grown up in a family that was well off, the living conditions in the park repulsed him. His childhood home was large and always clean. They never had to worry about food or money. He always had nice, freshly laundered clothes. When he first met Holly, he realized she had the same sort of upbringing, right down to the loving family members. He had been treated as one of their own from the first time he met her parents and he assumed, even with Monica leaving home at such a young age, that she would want the same type of lifestyle she had grown to know, even if it wasn't with her family close by.

Before he could change his mind, he knocked on the door. The hinges were so weak, the door knocked back into his fist. He heard rustling coming from inside before the door swung open. He stepped out of the way, narrowly avoiding it slamming into his shoulder.

"Can I help you?"

Greg's mouth hung open in shock and he closed it again before he could get any words out. He expected to find a woman down on her luck with dirty, ripped clothing, unwashed hair, and deep purple circles under her eyes. The woman standing before him was stunning, nothing at all like the female Holly and her mother had described to him. He had seen pictures of Monica and Holly together as teenagers. Being twins, they looked exactly alike, but the way Monica carried herself set them miles apart. It was clear to him now that time had been good to Monica and as much as he believed his wife to be beautiful, Monica was the one who shined. She must have put all her money into her physical appearance rather than her home.

After the initial shock wore off, he introduced himself to her and explained, briefly, why he was there. Holly may have been wrong about Monica's appearance, but she was spot on with her personality. She was as mean and vicious as Holly said she was. Every word that came out of her mouth was cold and she made it clear she had no desire to speak to or see her sister nor did she want to speak about her.

Knowing how much it would mean to Holly, Greg was going to be persistent. Holly was willing to set aside all their differences and the past for a chance to reconnect with Monica, to have a conversation with her. She wanted her sister to be a part of her life, no matter how small that part may be and Greg was going to do his best to make that happen. He gave up easily the first day, hoping Monica would take some time to think about her sister and realize how much it meant to her if Greg were willing to come all the way out here. Maybe she would be more receptive to him the next day. His goal was to fly back to Maryland with Monica so he could reunite the two sisters.

The following afternoon, just before one, he showed up on her doorstep, or rather cinder block steps, with half a dozen yellow roses in hand hoping it would show her he was serious about the two of them speaking. He thought about calling her before showing up uninvited two days in a row, but he was worried she might leave or outright refuse to speak to him. If he were standing directly in front of her, she wouldn't have a choice. When she opened the door, which surprised him in itself, he was just as shocked as he had been the first time. There was something about her looks that almost paralyzed him. She dressed in a thin sweater and tight jeans, emerald-green heels gave a pop of color to her outfit and made her almost the same height as him. He pushed the flowers toward her, like a teenager on a first date. He forgot to speak for a moment. When he finally did, he stuttered through an apology for showing up unannounced the day before.

"I was hoping we could talk. Can I come in?"

Monica stepped back so he had enough room to enter. He was disgusted by the way her home looked and the smell created a feeling of nausea that wormed its way from his stomach to his throat. Without looking, he knew the sink held dishes that were days old and the trash was most likely overflowing, if not from the garbage itself, then from a pulsing blanket of maggots coating the rim. She gestured toward the sofa for him to sit down but instead, he opted for a wooden stool that stood against the kitchen counter. He was concerned about sitting on a fabric piece of furniture that looked as though dust was the only thing holding it together. Seeing Monica standing in front of him, makeup, hair, and clothing pristine, she looked as out of place in this environment as he felt.

"I wanted to apologize for yesterday. I know I caught you off guard by just showing up on your doorstep, but I was afraid if I called you first, you would have refused to talk to me."

"I would have." She was direct in her answer and the annoyance of him showing up a second time showed on her face. "Thanks for the flowers, though. Maybe they'll brighten up the place. It could use something."

Greg looked toward the floor and mumbled under his breath, "A match might do it." He made eye contact again by drawing his eyes slowly up her body. "I know you seemed very adamant about your position when it came to seeing Holly, but I would really like it if you would at least hear me out." He waited for her to answer but she just stared at him with her arms crossed. Since she didn't cut him off, he took it as a sign to go ahead and say what he came here to say.

He told her about all the good things Holly had to say about her and Monica snickered in a way that told him she didn't believe any of it. "I know the two of you had a lot of problems with each other growing up but whether you believe it or not, Holly really does love you. She wants nothing more than to have some sort of relationship with you. If I had to guess, she would probably be okay with exchanging Christmas cards, anything that would ease you back into her life. And I know without a doubt, she would love to for you to meet our daughter." He waited to see if the mention of a child would spark any sign of emotion in her face. Digging into his back pocket, he retrieved his wallet and flipped it open. "Can I at least show you a picture of your niece?" He fumbled with the flimsy plastic holder her photo was stuck inside. "I know I'm biased but she really is cute."

Monica rolled her eyes but reached out her hand to take the photo from him. When their hands touched, they both lingered for a moment too long and something passed between them. Monica smirked.

Greg quickly withdrew his hand and chastised himself. What was he doing? This was his wife's sister. "Will you at least consider flying back with me? Take a few days and think about it?" His words didn't say it, but his eyes gave him away. He was pleading with her.

She didn't want to admit it but the look in his eyes had an impact. Not the kind that made her all warm and fuzzy but the kind that made her realize how easy it would be to manipulate him. She hated her sister with everything that she had and she fully intended to take what was rightfully hers. "I'll think about it but don't get your hopes up." She said the word 'don't' with conviction. "I'm about ninety-nine percent sure I won't be going anywhere with you. I don't think I can ever forgive Holly for what she did to me when we were younger, whether she apologizes or not. She made my life hell and we were supposed to be the ones guiding and protecting one another. This wasn't a case of simple sibling rivalry; she treated me worse than all the people we went to school with and she should feel bad about it." She turned away for a moment, pacing, and then turned back. "I can't help but feel like she just wants to see me so she can rub it in my face that she has everything that I don't. It's the way it's always been between the two of us. Perfect little Holly and the screw up, Monica." She handed Greg back the picture. "The kid is cute, though."

"Thank you. Her name is Lauren. She's five."

"Yeah. So, I'll let you know what I decide." She made her way to the door and opened it.

Greg took that as her not-so-subtle way of telling him to get the hell out of her house and he stood to leave. "I'll leave you my card, my cell phone number is on it. Let me know what you decide to do. I'll be in town for a few more days." He slid a card out of his wallet and set it on the kitchen counter. He had to brush past her on his way out.

Monica's door slammed shut behind him.

Greg came on this trip with good intentions. He wanted, more than anything, to be able to reunite the sisters. It was the one thing Holly wanted that money couldn't provide. He spent so much time and money trying to track Monica down that he was excited about coming to meet her. He had made up a scenario in his mind that she would welcome the idea of seeing her sister again. He thought if he explained how much it would mean to Holly, she would give in even if she was unsure. He didn't expect her to be so cold and unwilling to try.

He took a cold shower when he got back to his four-star hotel, hoping to scrub away the clammy feeling on his skin and the smell that he was sure had latched on to his clothing and crawled through his hair. Feeling refreshed, he laid in bed even though it was the middle of the day. His mind wandered, wondering first how long she would make him wait to hear her decision, and then to the curves of her body, the gentle sway of her hips when she turned away from him. He pulled his thoughts back and tried to think about what he would do if she said 'no.' Should he tell Holly he found her and she declined his invitation to visit? Should he play dumb and do his best to pretend he didn't know anything like he had for the last ten years since they met? But he did know something now. He knew how alluring Monica was, how confidently she carried herself. His hand trailed down his chest, outside his boxer briefs, feeling himself stir beneath the fabric. He lingered for a moment and then moved his hand under the waistband and grabbed ahold before standing and letting out a guttural moan. He shouldn't be having these thoughts. It was his wife's sister. Monica had made it perfectly clear she wanted nothing to do with him, but he struggled with his thoughts late into the night.

He wasted the following day exploring the city, waiting to hear back from Monica. He only had two days left and he was dreading the possibility of going home without her. He stopped on his way back to the hotel to purchase a sandwich and a six pack of beer. He didn't have any plans for the evening except to kick back and watch a few movies. He felt bad that Holly wasn't here to enjoy his time off with him, but he did feel that he needed a break from work. It was nice to get away from his daily routine and not have anything to worry about. He loved Holly and Lauren but when he was home, even away from work, he felt he never had any time for himself.

After he settled for the evening, he cracked open a beer and laid back on his pillows, flipping through channels to find something to watch. His cell phone buzzed and he sighed, assuming it was Holly saying 'hello.' He grabbed his phone off the nightstand and was pleasantly surprised. It wasn't Holly after all. It was Monica.

I MADE A DECISION. COME TALK TO ME.

Greg was a bit put out that he had just settled in his hotel for the evening, but he was anxious to hear what she had to say, equally nervous that she made the decision so fast. He had a nagging feeling it was not going to go in the direction he was hoping for. He slid his shoes back on, put his beer in the mini refrigerator, and left the room.

His heart was pounding as he approached Monica's door. He thought, even if she said 'no,' she might be close enough to the edge that he would be able to convince her. He knocked on the door and heard her yell that it was open. He opened the door cautiously and poked his head in. He didn't immediately see Monica but once he stepped inside, he saw more of her than he was expecting. She was lying on the couch, wearing a sheer nightgown. The leg furthest away, straight out, the closest bent at the knee so the nightie fell just below her buttock. Her hair splayed on the pillow under her head and the lace trim cut just above her nipples. He knew he should leave but the sight of her lying there held him in place.

"So, I haven't fully made my decision yet, but I was thinking you might be able to convince me to go back with you if you play your cards right." Her eyes held a devilish look and traced the folds of the satin fabric with her finger as she spoke.

"Ahh... I don't think... Maybe I should go... I can't..."

She chuckled a little at his reply and stood to walk over to him. She ran her hand down his chest and whispered in his ear. "Come on, Greg. You can't deny that you would love the chance to sleep with your wife's twin. It's a fantasy of many men and so few can say they lived it." She grabbed the top of his waistband. "I don't know how much Holly told you but the two of us have always been competitive and I would love the chance to show you that I am much, much better than her at some things." She gently licked the area behind his ear and kissed his lips in a teasing manner. "You do want me to fly back with you, don't you? Convince me." She grabbed his hand and walked him back to her bedroom.

She stood with her back to the bed and pulled him close. With both hands she began unbuttoning his shirt. "Even when you're not working, you still dress the part." She shook her head. "Let's see if we can get you to relax a little bit."

Greg didn't protest, he didn't put up a fight. He hadn't played this exact scenario in his head, but he felt as if it were a continuation of his thoughts from the previous night, a daydream rather than reality. And he wanted it. After two rounds and a shortened third, he told Monica he had to go.

Exhaustion settled over him as he sat in his car. His skin was sticky with sweat and he turned the air on full blast. He waited while waves of excitement and remorse took turns washing over him. Before leaving the pull-off, he checked his phone and saw he had eight missed messages from Holly. He responded quickly, apologizing, and telling her he had fallen asleep when he got back to the hotel. He felt awful about the lie.

He collapsed onto the bed but laid awake for hours, replaying his evening with Monica. When he awoke the next day, he couldn't get her out of his head. He drank some hot coffee and took a cold shower, tried to plan something to do for the day. In the end, he gave up and drove back to Monica's. As soon as she opened the door, he pushed her inside and barely had time to close the door before she was naked again.

Afterward, they both sat at the counter drinking iced tea and Greg told her what time the flight left the next day. The thought never crossed his mind that she would say 'no' now.

"About that, Greg. I've decided not to go. I mean, don't get me wrong, you are certainly convincing in some areas, but I still don't have any desire to have a relationship with my sister. If you're ever in town again, you know where to find me."

Greg sat there, stunned. He had no idea what to say. The only benefit he could see was that he wouldn't have to sit in the same room with both of them after what he had done but he thought they had a deal; he slept with her, she flew back with him.

"So, I gave you my answer. Is there anything else you wanted or was that it??" She asked the question as she walked to her door and opened it. Greg realized she was dismissing him again and he had nothing left to say. He walked out with silence hanging in the air between them.

# Chapter 21

## Time Does Not Heal Open Wounds

Holly sat on the edge of her bed with a blanket wrapped around her, her heart and brain pulling her emotions in different directions. She wasn't sure she could trust Paige, but she kept trying to remind herself that she was only a child. She leaned forward and pulled Lauren's framed photo from the drawer in her nightstand. Tears sprung to her eyes as her fingers traced the outline of her daughter's face. She wondered, if Lauren were here today, would she feel the same way about Paige? Would she trust her more if she had a better understanding of how teenagers worked, if she had been witness to the transition from childhood into young adult?

She hugged the photo to her chest, trying to remember what it was like to feel Lauren's arms wrapped around her. Every day, the memories seemed to fade a little further away, like a dream one only remembers in bits and pieces, nothing makes sense and no two pieces fit together. She still felt the two years after the accident, living with her husband in a state of coexistence, sleeping in separate beds, speaking only when necessary, never touching. Their love for each other never changed, but the ability to put their emotions into words was far out of reach.

Holly's mind tortured her, scattering memories of her daughter through others' actions and words, never forming a full picture. Haunted only by the phone call she received that night; she remembers perfectly and yet doesn't feel she was there. Tears spilled down her cheeks.

Greg came into the bedroom and wrapped his arms around her. She pulled the photo away from her chest and turned it so he could see. "I have trouble remembering her face sometimes."

He pulled her closer. "Me too."

The memory of Lauren's last night pulled Greg in. He waited for Lauren at the kitchen table. Her school was hosting a daddy-daughter kindergarten carnival. She had been talking about it for weeks. Every child had some form of artwork displayed at the fair and Lauren, being above average in the arts, got to paint a backdrop for the balloon pop game consisting of a large clown face that would show once the participants popped all the balloons. The only hint she would give Greg about her project was that her painting had blue hair. They played a game all week with Greg trying to guess what she had painted.

The night of the carnival, Lauren bounced down the hall and into the kitchen wearing a curly, multi-colored wig.

"Well, don't you look dressed for the part. Are you ready to go?"

Lauren shook her head and reached up, pressing her palms against the wig to straighten it. "I have a surprise, but you have to close your eyes."

"Okay. They're closed."

"Don't peek." She reached into her pocket and pulled out a red, foam nose which she attached to her own with precision. "Okay, open them."

Greg opened his eyes and looked at her. He leaned to the side to look behind her and then peered under the table before looking at her again. "Where'd Lauren go?"

She exploded into one of her infectious giggles and clawed the nose from her face. "I'm right here, Daddy."

He dropped his lower jaw and faked a gasp. "You tricked me." He picked her up and threw her half over his shoulder before leaning down to kiss Holly goodbye.

"Have fun you two." She watched as they left the house. She loved seeing the two of them together and equally loved having some time to herself. Holly lost herself in a book for the next two hours until the phone pulled her from her adventure.

Over the phone, they wouldn't give her any information, but she wasn't sure she would have understood it even if they did. The only words she remembered from the call were: accident, presence requested, hospital. She's still not sure how she got to the hospital. She stayed with Greg for two days, alternating between his room and the waiting room down the hall, going home only to shower and change her clothes. While she was with Greg, she refused to accept that Lauren was gone and didn't believe anything the doctors told her. Greg stayed in the hospital five days and they scheduled Lauren's funeral for two weeks after their accident.

Holly remained numb until that day. For most, saying goodbye allows them to begin the healing process. For her, it was the opposite, all stages of grief came at once. Holly directed her anger at Greg and she blamed him for the loss of their daughter. She asked him numerous times over the next two years to move out of the house, but he refused. He would never leave her and he also didn't trust her on her own. Holly wouldn't eat, Greg all but dragged her into the bathroom to take a shower. She was on an extended leave of absence and Greg had to hire a home health care aide and a psychiatrist to keep watch over her when he went back to work.

It hurt Greg deeply that she blamed him, but he understood her emotional state. He blamed himself, too. Deep down, he knew it wasn't solely his fault, but he was driving. He drove his car off the road when a deer ran out in front of them. That was the story and that's what he told people. The part he had left out for the last thirteen years was that his distraction was due to an argument with Lauren. For the second time that week, Lauren had been carrying on about seeing her mother when they were out when Greg knew Holly was at home.

The first time, Lauren let the conversation drop easily. The night of the accident, she wouldn't let it go. The school was a thirteen-minute drive from their house and ten minutes in she had taken to crying, screaming, and kicking the seat in front of her. Greg had enough of her meltdown and turned back to yell at her. That moment was all it took. In three seconds, Greg's life had changed forever. He lost his only child, sent his wife into an emotional breakdown, and would be guilt ridden for the rest of his days about his last words to his child. Like his father before him, Greg turned his head and loudly proclaimed, "Lauren, enough. Stop crying or I'll give you something to cry about."

Never did he imagine those words to be so true and so false at the same time. He did give her something to cry about but Lauren would never cry again.

# Chapter 22

## Finally Free

Monica had never been able to live up to the standards Holly created. She was consistently the underdog in everything and everyone in her life reminded her of that fact every day. Holly was in advanced classes in school which meant she typically had teachers a full year before Monica did. Seeing her name on their roster, they were all excited to meet her, believing she would excel the same way Holly did. Once they found out she was nothing like Holly, they wanted nothing more to do with her. Even when Monica put her best efforts forward and showed she was trying, the teachers didn't care. Every day she heard something close to the phrase *"Why can't you be more like your sister? She was so good at this."* She couldn't understand why no one was able to figure out that she wasn't Holly. She would never be like Holly. But that didn't make her a bad person or any worse than her sister, they were just different. They were different because they were actually two different people.

They didn't get along from the very beginning and nothing changed as they got older. Holly had always been into makeup and nice clothes, she prided herself on her appearance. She always wanted their mother to fix her hair and she would cry if she chipped her nail polish. Monica preferred to play outside all day, not a care in the world if she had dirt under her fingernails or grass stains on the knees of her pants. Holly liked dolls and learning how to cook while Monica wanted to feel her adrenaline pumping by riding anything with wheels, she had zero priorities and would choose lounging on the couch all day to anything that required learning. Holly put time into her studies and locked herself in her room as soon as she got home from school to do homework and study. Monica stayed out with friends and came home just in time to go to bed. As teenagers, they didn't even listen to the same type of music. Holly, being the perfect teenage girl, listened to popular alternative hits and dance songs while Monica preferred heavier music, grunge and metal.

On the rare occasion they were all in the same room together, if Holly had music playing on the radio, their mother would dance and even sing along at times. If Monica put her music on, their mother would always refer to it as 'trash' and tell her to 'turn that noise off.' It was always little things like that but as a child and a teenager, hearing it every day begins to wear on someone. How often can someone hear they aren't good enough or they should be more like someone else? Monica never felt as though she had support from anyone. She didn't get support from her parents, her teachers, or even her twin sister. All Holly seemed to care about was herself and pleasing everyone else around her. Monica thought Holly liked her being the problem child because it made her look better.

The day Monica made the decision to leave their childhood home, Holly found out she was the valedictorian of their class. An announcement came over the intercom at school and everyone in Monica's class turned to stare at her. One of Holly's friends glared at her and said, "Gonna be hard to live up to that, huh, Shags?" Her comment caused the entire room to laugh. 'Shags' was a nickname given to her all the way back in middle school having to do with her shaggy hair and baggy clothes. Even Holly had taken to calling her that until their mother made her stop. It wasn't because she felt differently, it was just to pretend she was playing fair. Monica knew better, she always did. Her mother had been trying to get her to change her looks for years. She would buy her new sweaters or a new shirt and Monica would hang them up in the closet until they found their way to the back, never to see light again. No one, including her parents, understood that she wasn't going to change just because they wanted her to. After the announcement at the school, people were coming up to Monica all day asking her if she was proud of her sister and wondering what she was going to do to compare to that. Her teachers all relayed the same message being *'If you were more like your sister, that could be you.'* By the time she left school for the day she had had enough.

She decided for the first time all year to go home directly after school so she wouldn't have to deal with hearing any of her friends talking about Holly. She knew her friends would have her back and they would never ask her why they were so different, but she didn't want to talk about Holly at all. She just wanted to go home, lock herself away in her bedroom, and wallow in her own sorrow. As soon as she walked into the house, the chaos began. Her grandmother was already there sitting on the couch, one of her aunts was standing in the living room, no doubt having started her drinking around noon, and Monica knew right away she had made the wrong decision by coming home. Her mother called to her and forced her into the kitchen to mingle with the growing crowd. Before she said anything to anyone else, she turned to her mother to ask, "How did you get this many people here on such short notice? This is insane. Would her graduation party not have been enough?"

Her mother grabbed her by the back of her arm and squeezed. "Do not make a scene, Monica.

This is very important celebration for your sister, she has earned this. It's no one's fault but your own that people are here to celebrate her accomplishments and not yours. Maybe you should remember that the next time you decide to skip class or stay out most of the night. I don't know where I went wrong with you, but you will not screw this up for your sister. You should be proud of her and what she has achieved. Now, go chat with your grandma and your aunt. And for the love of God, please go put on some appropriate clothes. You look like a mess."

Monica was raging mad. Of all people, her mother should be the one to take it easy on her and try to understand how this all might make her feel. Instead, she proved herself to be the worst one of all. Monica turned, groaning as she did so, with a plan of going upstairs and not coming back down until she was sure everyone was gone. She was sure no one would miss her. As she swung around, she ran straight into Holly.

"Well, sister, I guess this has to be a pretty shitty day for you, huh?" One side of her mouth turned up in a sneering grin.

Monica stepped back, took a deep breath, and pushed Holly backwards, hard. Three people jumped toward her to hold her back from causing any further harm. Her mother screamed at her for making a scene and embarrassing her sister. Without thinking twice about it, Monica turned around and swung her arm, connecting her fist directly with her mother's face. She stood still for a moment, in shock at her own level of violence, and then ran out the back door. She bent over, with her hands on her knees, trying to catch her breath and keep from crying before sitting on the top step of the back porch.

Every person in the kitchen must have thought she ran far away because not a single person came out to check on her. All anyone could focus on was Holly falling backward. With nothing more than a screen door between them, Monica sat on that step and listened to all the comments and snippets of conversation coming from the kitchen.

NOBODY AT SCHOOL LIKES HER.
PEOPLE CAN'T EVEN BELIEVE WE'RE
RELATED.
WHY DOES SHE DRESS LIKE THAT?
SHE DOES IT TO HERSELF.
IT'S HER OWN FAULT FOR NOT PUSHING
HERSELF HARDER.
I'VE TRIED TO MAKE HER MORE PRESENTABLE,
BUT SHE WON'T COOPERATE.
I DON'T KNOW HOW I MANAGED TO SCREW UP
SO BAD WITH THAT ONE.

The last bit of conversation coming from her mother was the end of it for her. She decided right then she was leaving her house and she wouldn't come back. It was obvious to her, no one in her family was going to fight for her, including her own mother.

# Chapter 23

## The Zoo

Lucy ran toward the monkey exhibit. She had already visited the tigers and the giraffes. As much as she loved them, the monkeys were her favorite. She found one hidden in the corner and she stood in front of it, making hand gestures and sticking her tongue out, trying to get it to imitate her movements. She put her hands on top of her head, fingers splayed like moose antlers, and saw a reflection behind her in the glass. She jumped up and down and turned with a big smile grin on her face. "Hi Mom...oh, hi Aunt Monica."

Monica flashed her sweetest smile. "Hi, Lucy. What are you doing here?"

"I'm on a field trip for school. Why are you here?"

"I came to see," she looked in the glass area to figure out what display she had come up on, "the monkeys. They're my favorite."

Lucy's smile covered half her face. "Mine, too. I'm trying to get them to play 'monkey-see, monkey-do.'"

"That's the best animal to play it with."

"Do you want to try with me?"

"Sure. I'll copy you and maybe the monkey will copy both of us."

"Okay." Lucy turned back toward the monkey, put her arms out to the side, and started doing a little jig. She giggled when she saw Monica following her movements. The monkey turned and ran away and Lucy shrugged. "Maybe he doesn't like dancing."

"I guess not. His loss. Do you want to go sit on the bench with me for a minute?"

"Okay, but I'd rather watch the monkeys."

"Let's talk for a minute and we'll come back to see them again." She led the way to the cement bench and sat down. "Do you remember our secret from the last time we saw each other?"

Lucy nodded enthusiastically. "Uh huh. I can't tell mommy and daddy that we talked to each other because they don't like you very much."

"That's right. You have a good memory."

"Thanks."

"I'm glad I saw you today. Paige told me that someone hurt you a couple of weeks ago. What happened?"

She stuck her bottom lip out. "Yeah, I got hurt in my sleep. I had a really big black and blue right on my eye."

"Oh, no. That must have hurt a lot. Do you remember what happened?"

Lucy shrugged. "I think mommy hit me. I don't remember though because I was sleeping."

"Why do you think it was your mom?" She pulled her jacket tighter around her.

"She told me I was dreaming. But I remember her calling my name like she does when I have to get up for school. I was really sleepy and it was hard for me to open my eyes."

"Did you see her in your room?"

"Uh huh. But only for a minute. I just wanted to go back to sleep."

Monica was so glad she remembered seeing her. "That must have been scary." She watched while Lucy nodded. "Lucy, has anyone talked to you about it? If someone is hurting you, you should find an adult to tell."

"I told you."

"You did. But tell someone who can help you. Maybe a teacher at school, or a neighbor."

"Lucy? Who are you talking to?" Her teacher was approaching them from the back of the bench. "Lucy?"

"Remember to keep our secret. Don't tell anyone we talked, okay?"

"Okay." Lucy nodded and faced her teacher. "Hi, Mrs. Long. I was watching the monkeys."

# Chapter 24

### If I Can't Have It...

Paige was homesick and she couldn't figure out why. She hated her home life and often felt more comfortable sleeping under a park bench or beside a dumpster in an alley. She left her mother's house four months ago and until now, she hadn't missed it at all. It could be the weather that hadn't wanted to cooperate the past week. It was cold and raining, when the rain stopped, the dampness still hung in the air and the chill didn't want to go away. When she left, not by her own choice, her mother's boyfriend had just moved in with his daughter. Paige didn't get along with either of them. Knowing her mother's track record, she thought by this time, the man and his daughter would be long gone.

One thing she had learned being on her own was to never sleep in the same place twice, it made it easy to become a victim of theft or assault.

Keeping herself on the move, she had made it three towns over in the past four months and spent three days walking back home. As soon as she hit the town limits, her body surged with adrenaline, excited to see her mother again, hoping she might be able to sleep with a roof over her head. She knew better but still held out hope that her mother might be excited to see her as well. When she got to the house, she crept along the bushes in her neighbor's yard. The brown grass, in need of mowing, wrapped around her ankles and the mud sucked at the soles of her shoes. The front of her house was the same. It hadn't seen a lawnmower in months and the lawn had bits of trash and papers scattered across it. The wood siding was rotting and split and one shingle had fallen off, taking up residence on the ground below. The roof of the carport was sagging at the corner due to a broken support beam. To an outsider, it wouldn't be a welcome sight, but to Paige, it was a place to call home.

She knew her neighbors wouldn't be home for a few more hours so she stayed behind the bushes, waiting for her mother's car to pull into the driveway. For two hours, she shifted between crouching and kneeling, her jeans soaking up the mud and water, cold seeping into her skin. She was ready to give up, to find a place to warm up when she saw a car coming up the street. She saw her mother driving when the vehicle turned into the driveway, along with a man in the passenger seat.

Once parked, she realized it was the same man her mother was dating when she left. His daughter peeled herself out of the back seat and Paige's heart sank. She wanted to reconnect with her mother, but she didn't want to face her when the other two were home.

Disheartened, she waited for them to make their way inside before going back to the shops in town to scope out a place to sleep. The following four days, she got comfortable on the corner of the lawn between the two houses, waiting for the other two to leave her mother alone. Day after day, Paige was disappointed to see the three of them always seemed to travel together. On the fourth night, she thought she had gotten lucky when she saw the girl come outside by herself and slide into the passenger's seat of the Oldsmobile. Her excitement diminished quickly when she saw, not the man, but her mother leave the house with her purse hooked over her shoulder and the car keys in her hand. Watching her mother drive away with another child in her car made Paige's heart sink. She felt all the emotions she experienced the day her mother kicked her out coming back again. Tears stung her eyes and she hung her head, embarrassed by her own naivety. *Why would she think her mother wanted anything to do with her?* It was now clear to Paige that she had moved on. She stood to leave and heard a door slam behind her. Her mother's boyfriend, Jim, left the house and walked down the street in the opposite direction.

She didn't know how long he would be gone, but knowing the house was empty, Paige marched up to the house, walked around to the back, and pried open her old bedroom window. Knowing she wouldn't be getting the reunion she hoped for, she refused to make this a wasted trip. Hoisting herself up by the ledge, she propelled herself through the window, tumbling to the floor below. It took her eyes a moment to adjust to the dim lighting and the smell of dampness and mold made her lip curl. She wanted to scream. Looking around the room she noticed someone had removed all her stuff. Her bed, dresser, clothes, everything was gone. She stormed out of her old room and walked into the living room. As she expected, the one photo of her that hung over the fireplace was gone. Replacing it was a family portrait of her mother, Jim, and his daughter. Screaming, she grabbed the nearest lamp and threw it against the photo, ripping the cord out of the wall. The glass in the frame shattered and rained down over the stained carpet. She swung the front door open and ran down the street as fast as her feet allowed.

Tears trailed down her face as she ran. Instead of tears of sadness and hurt, they had transformed into those of anger and hatred. Her eyes, throat, and lungs burned from the mix of tears and chilly weather. *How had her mother moved on so fast?* Paige had never felt this level of anger and she finally understood the meaning of the phrase, 'seeing red.' She had heard the expression before but didn't realize the extent of how accurate it was. She stopped running and leaned against a tree trunk, palms on her knees, trying to catch her breath. She wanted to scream and cry and throw a tantrum, but she knew it wouldn't do any good, it wouldn't make her feel better. What would make her feel better was the revenge she believed her mother deserved.

Paige found a dark alley with a picnic table butted against a brick wall. She shook out her thin, fleece blanket and laid it under the table just as it started to drizzle. It was a little early to lay down, still too many people walking around, but she wanted a quiet place to think. It rained all night and Paige watched as heavy, wet snowflakes mixed with the rain drops. Thankful for the shelter of the table over her head, it didn't do any good keeping her blanket dry. After a restless night, she gathered the few belongings she owned and was on the move before the sun was up. She was running on adrenaline, ready to take away all her mother's possessions as quickly as her mother was to get rid of hers.

She walked fast to get out some of the energy she had coursing through her system. She didn't want to attract any unwanted attention to herself. She needed to keep a low profile for the day. It was still early so she took a detour to the park in the center of town so she could wash her face in the fountain before the joggers started their morning routine. Just after eight, she arrived at the small, locally run general store in the next town over. She knew a lot of people would enter the store when it opened and that's what she wanted, to be able to blend in with the crowd. Before she entered, she ducked around the corner of the building to count the coins in her pocket. She wanted to make sure, if someone started to question her presence, she had enough to buy a bottle of water to give her a reason to be there.

Her stomach growled and she reminded herself that she wasn't going in for food. She had two items she needed and she needed to focus on them. The hard part was, she knew, the store kept both items stored near the register so she would have to wait until a small line formed. The way they arranged the store, she had a perfect view of the registers from the front of the store. She leaned against the brick and waited until a small line formed. The wind had picked up while she waited and a chill ran through her. Her clothes were still damp from the rain and snow overnight. When the next person opened the door to go in, she followed so the bell above the door wouldn't chime a second time. She walked directly to the other side of the register, looking around to make sure no one was watching her, and pocketed the first item she needed. She had to scan the area for a moment before she found the other item she needed. She walked to the counter and leaned her back against it, making sure to keep her head down. In a hushed voice she asked, "Excuse me, Sir? Can you tell me where the bus station is?" She waited for the man to turn and look at her. "I've been walking for an hour and can't seem to find it." She hoped the tone of her voice would gain sympathy rather than curiosity.

He cocked his head to the side, scrunched his face, and gave her the simplest directions. Paige knew she was taking a chance by asking about the bus station because she knew it was right around the corner. She had spent a few nights there over the past few years. While he was speaking, she balled her fists behind her back and as soon as he turned back to the register, she pocketed the second item and squeaked out a "thank you" before leaving the store.

She walked two blocks before stopping to slow her heart rate. No matter how many times she went into a store and stole something, the nervous feeling that someone was going to catch her never went away. While she might entertain the idea of having a pillow and blanket to sleep on and a warm place to stay, she didn't like the idea of going to jail for longer than a night. When she felt comfortable that no one was coming after her, she set out to go to her mother's house. Paige wanted to keep watch of the house so she could see whenever someone left. She didn't want to stay as close as she had the past few days, it was too risky. Seeing her mother's car in the driveway, she was hopeful that meant she would be leaving later tonight.

As soon as that thought entered her head, she saw the front door open and her mother stepped out wearing only a thin, T-shirt style nightgown. It was the first time Paige had gotten a good look at her since she started watching the house. She looked much older than her thirty-odd years. Her hair was slack and graying around her face, the bags under her eyes were thick and heavy and her skin sagged over her fragile frame. For a moment, Paige felt a tugging at her heart, remembering how her mother treated her when she first moved in. She had felt so loved and protected; she never would have thought her mother would turn out to be the person she is. The moment passed quickly and the loving feeling dissipated. Paige had a mission to accomplish and reminiscing about the past wasn't going to stop her.

For hours, Paige was shaking and sweating. The sun had come out and dried her clothes, but it wasn't warm and she didn't know if her symptoms were due to nerves, anger, or a combination of the two. She kept an eye on the house all day and as dusk approached, she hid behind a tree that bordered the neighbor's yard. It wasn't the best place to hide but as long as she didn't do anything to attract attention, she should be able to remain there without anyone seeing her. She stayed crouched for nearly an hour and her legs were cramping from the position. Just as she was about to move, light spilled out from the front door of the house and the family of three came out, chitchatting on their way to the car.

She waited ten minutes to make sure they weren't coming back, quickly made her way around the back of the house and vaulted through the same window as the day before. Her first mission was to raid the kitchen and get as much food as she could store in her bag. She emptied boxes of fruit snacks, crackers, and trail mix, and threw some mini boxes of cereal into her bag before making her way down the hall to the girl's room. Paige figured they were about the same size so she pulled clothes from her closet and dresser without looking at them. She took a blanket from her bed and tied it around the straps of her backpack. She dropped the bag slowly out the window and glanced back, making sure there was nothing else she could use. Once she was satisfied she had everything she needed, she dangled her feet out the window, holding herself up with her torso and elbows. She pulled the plastic bottle of lighter fluid from her pocket and squirted it across the room as far as it would go. She already dumped some in the kitchen and down the hall. Being sure to douse the bed sheets and pillow, she sprayed the fluid until the bottle was empty. She tossed the empty container into the middle of the room and slid out the window. Removing the lighter from her pocket, she picked up a t-shirt she had grabbed from the closet and squirted lighter fluid on and held the flame close. Once it caught fire, she tossed the shirt through the window and watched until she could see the flames rising above the window ledge. Grabbing her backpack, she ran as fast as she could away from the house. She stopped and leaned against a fence, trying to catch her breath and calm her nerves. Sirens sounded in the distance and it brought a wave of relief over her until a hand grabbed at her arm and pulled at her.

"Shh," Monica whispered as she dragged Paige away from the open area she was resting in. "Come with me." Paige followed her, half-unwillingly, to a more secluded spot in the neighborhood. "What you just did...was very stupid. Do you know how easily you could have gotten caught?"

"I didn't get caught."

Monica looked at her with an expression that said, 'you're kidding me, right?' The words that came out of her mouth were slightly more gentle. "I caught you. What were you thinking?" She tightened the grip she had on Paige's arm.

"I don't have to explain myself to you. I'm leaving." She twisted her body to free her arm.

"Whoa. Hold on, just a second. One, do you have any idea how much trouble I can get you in? And two, I can help you if you lose the attitude."

Paige swung around to face her again. She was scared but it came out as anger. "How much trouble you can get me in? You have no idea who I am."

"Honey, I've been following you all day. I watched you at the store this morning. I saw you, clear as day, pocket the lighter and the lighter fluid. I followed you all the way to that house you just destroyed and I watched you all day while you watched the house. You had no idea I was there. Do you really think I won't be able to find you again? You don't really think it's a coincidence that we keep running into each other, do you?" She stood straight with her arms crossed, daring Paige to argue with her.

Now Paige knew why her nerves were acting up all day. She did feel like someone was watching her, but she never saw anyone. "What do you want from me?"

Monica set her palms on Paige's shoulders. "That depends on whether you trust me or not." She shrugged. "I need your help and you need a place to stay. What do you say?"

Paige snarled at her. "I have a place to stay, thank you. Right now, I just want to get out of here." She started to walk away and Monica grabbed her arm again.

"Didn't I just tell you I've been watching you all day? You absolutely do not have a place to stay." She put her hand up to stop Paige from speaking when she saw her mouth open. "Your clothes are filthy, you filled up your backpack while you were inside the house and I can only assume you took food and clothes. And you have a blanket that you didn't have when you went in. No one that has a place to stay would do that." She loosened her grip on her arm, hoping she wouldn't run. "So, you can either trust me or you can run away but I guarantee, you will get caught." She stared at Paige while she was waiting for her to answer. After a full thirty seconds, she saw Paige's body relax and she knew she had made up her mind.

"Fine," Paige finally replied. "I'll come with you."

# Chapter 25

## Some Days Slap You in the Face…with a Brick

ARE YOU SURE YOU WANT
TO LET YOUR ONLY REMAINING
DAUGHTER GET IN A CAR ALONE WITH HIM?

Holly's breath caught in her throat and watched her phone tumble through air, slow motion, and bounce on the carpet. No one knew the details of the accident except the responding officers. Holly and Greg promised each other they wouldn't give anyone specific details. Before her breakdown, she made Greg promise not to say anything. She didn't want anyone to blame him for what happened. She tried to remember if it was possible that she mentioned it to someone. For two years, she had trouble remembering anything that happened.

A ringing began in her ears and she felt like someone was slicing into her brain with a searing hot butcher's knife. Her vision blurred and she rested her face in her hands. She hadn't realized she was crying until she felt the wetness coating her cheeks.

Holly returned from her therapy appointment not feeling any better than before she went. She was no stranger to the therapy days, not knowing how she would feel when she left. Therapy was designed to make one relive, discuss, and accept events that occurred while simultaneously helping that person to move forward. Holly learned years ago there was a fair amount of give and take. She remembered the days she would leave her appointment, feeling like she could conquer the world and the same number of days leaving the office and hiding under her blankets until the next morning. Today was that type of day.

Her therapist, Bonnie, told her to ignore the message and block the number. Holly didn't care who the unknown number belonged to. She tried to argue that this person could be the answer to everything that had been happening to her, but Bonnie thought it would be more detrimental to her fragile emotional state. Sitting in her bedroom, Holly took a screenshot before deleting the message. She couldn't bring herself to block the number. Something was nagging at her, telling her a future message may hold some clue that would be helpful to her.

She fought with herself for hours, torn between showing Greg the message or keeping it to herself. She stared at him as he drifted off to sleep, the urge to disturb him pulling at her. She should have said something, let him help her. Now, as his breathing slowed, she rested her head on her pillow, eyes wide open and a new subject entered her mind. Bonnie was good at what she did, so good that Holly couldn't lie to her. While she was at the office, Bonnie asked her if she was taking her medication and she had to tell the truth. Two weeks ago, she went into the bathroom to take it and couldn't find it in the medicine cabinet. The empty bottle was resting in the trash can. She had filled the prescription four days prior and wasn't eligible for a refill for another month.

Bonnie urged her to tell Greg, reminding her that the medication was important in keeping her mind clear and her thoughts focused. They were also a condition of her going back to work. If she wasn't taking her pills, her employer could fire her. Holly promised she would tell her husband, but she didn't. She knew he would try to blame her for the empty bottle somehow.

# Chapter 26

## Just a Casual Reminder

Everyone had just settled down for the evening. Holly sat in her favorite chair with her feet propped on the ottoman and a book in her hands. Lucy had a children's variety puzzle book and Paige had the children's laptop balanced on her lap. Greg had a local news channel playing quietly on the television while he sifted through a file folder of papers for work.

Every evening was the same on school nights. Holly was adamant about having some quiet time for Lucy before bed. Even though they hadn't enrolled Paige in school, the rule included her. Between seven and eight-thirty phones were off limits for everyone until Lucy went to bed.

Greg seemed to forget about the rules and his phone pinged from a text message. Everyone in the room stopped what they were doing and raised their eyes to him in slow motion. "Sorry. I must have forgotten to put it on silent." He didn't reach for his phone, believing it wouldn't happen again. He never got messages this late unless they were from Holly. Since she was in the same room, he went back to his paperwork, leaving his phone on the table.

Ten minutes later, his phone pinged again, Lucy sighed as a third message came through.

"Come on, Greg." Holly dropped her book on the end table and stood, reaching forward to grab his phone at the same time he did.

"I'll fix it." He turned the volume to silent and tried to discreetly check to see who was messaging him. The number showed as 'unknown.'

HAVE YOU TOLD HER YET, GREG?
OR ARE YOU WAITING FOR ME TO SAY
SOMETHING
?

He squinted, wondering what the message was referring to. If it weren't for the sender using his name, he would have assumed it was a wrong number. He had been so busy trying to decipher the message, he didn't notice Holly standing right in front of him. She reached her hand out and he pulled his phone to his chest. "I just wanted to check, make sure it wasn't an emergency."

Holly rolled her eyes. "Well, who was it?"

"Wrong number...in a group chat." He hesitated before adding, "I'm just going to remove myself from the chat now."

The last bit was enough to satisfy her and she sat back down as the next message came through.

DO YOU WANT TO COME SEE ME AGAIN?

A photo followed the question and contained a woman's torso, covered only with a sheer, black bra. Greg shifted uncomfortably while he closed his messaging app and turned his phone off. His face grew hot and he glanced at Holly, thankful she had gone back to reading. He was certain she could hear his heart pounding in his chest.

The next morning, while Holly showered, he powered his phone back on with the intention of replying to the messages, telling her he knew who she was. Three new messages appeared before he got the chance. The first was a full body shot, minus her face, in the same bra as the previous, this one with the sheer panties to match.

I MISS YOU.

The photo that followed almost made Greg drop his phone. It was the same full body as the last, this one missing the undergarments, just her hand covering barely the area where her panties had been.

He replied to the messages, asking her not to text him again and dropped his phone into his pocket.

# Chapter 27

## So Much for Confidentiality

Holly's phone pinged with an incoming message. A short grunt escaped her lips and she hoisted herself up from her pillow, reaching for her phone. Unknown. She opened the message and found an attached sound clip. Without thinking, she clicked on it and listened to the entire three minutes. Her throat tightened and her mouth watered like she was going to be sick. The clip was from her latest therapy session, the back and forth about her empty bottle of medication. She listened to the message twice, wondering how someone could have recorded her session. During the third time, her phone pinged with another message.

HAVE YOU CHECKED YOUR HUSBAND'S PHONE RECENTLY?

She set her phone down and slid off the side of bed, careful not to disturb Greg. Using the small lamp from her side table, she made her way around the bed, pausing to look at his face. Satisfied that he was still sleeping, she reached for his phone. Her body began to shake and her muscles weakened, her nerves taking over.

Holly and Greg had a trusting relationship. They didn't lock their phones or hide them from each other, but they also never went through the other's phone. They never felt a need to. She unplugged his phone from the charger, her heart pounding in her chest and made her way to her office. Scrolling through his messages, she found nothing unusual, his emails, including the trash folder, were the same. She breathed a sigh of relief, now certain whoever was sending those messages was just trying to mess with her head. She stood and walked toward the door, pausing right before the hallway. She woke up the phone again and clicked on the photo gallery. A vignette took over her vision. Two photos of Lucy and one of Lucy and Paige took over the top row. The rest of the screen was filled with photos of what appeared to be one woman, in various stages of undress. It reminded her of those little flip books from her childhood where a stick figure could be seen doing a cartwheel when you flipped the pages fast enough. She felt if she scrolled through the photos, she'd see the woman undressing before her eyes.

For a moment she felt as if her heart stopped beating, a hollow void filled her chest before her heart slammed against her ribcage again. She wouldn't wake him, but now she would have to tell him about the messages she was receiving and she would have to ask him about the photos. Tears stung her eyes as she made her way back to the bedroom. Her hands trembled as she tried to fit the charging cord into the phone. Every sound, including the rush of blood in her ears was amplified and she was sure Greg would wake at any moment. With the phone plugged in, she lay on the edge of the bed, just shy of sliding off, her eyes trained on the ceiling. She dozed off only once for a brief time and got out of bed before the sun came up.

# Chapter 28

### It's Inappropriate and Concerning

Martin stood inside the office, waiting for Holly to arrive.

"Good morning." She walked to her desk and put her bag inside the bottom drawer of the desk as she always does. She could feel his eyes on her, watching her, but he hadn't said anything yet. She powered on her computer and sat in her chair. He was still watching and it was making her uncomfortable. Are you okay this morning?" She turned to face him and noticed he had a look of distress she hadn't seen before. "What's wrong?"

"We need to talk. Come into the office." He turned his back and retreated into his office. His voice sounded different and set her nerves on edge. She followed him in and he pointed to the chair across from his desk. "Sit."

She felt like she was sitting in the principal's office because someone tattled on her. Martin wasn't speaking and the silence was unbearable. She was sure an hour of time had passed and she grew more uncomfortable by the minute. Her skin prickled and her muscles felt weak.

Martin put his elbows on the desk and steepled his fingers. "Holly, how long have we worked together?"

"Um, close to twenty years. I don't know exactly." Her heart started pounding.

"And in those years, you've been married the whole time, as have I. We had good, working relationship throughout those years, yes?"

"I've always thought so." She wanted to crawl out of her skin, scream at him to get to the point of what he wanted to say.

He sighed and dropped his hands, sat up straighter in his chair. "I'm sure I don't need to remind you that your employment here is conditional. I gave you another chance after a very extended leave when you were going through your...emotional troubles."

"I remember."

"And one of those conditions of you coming back was that you had to stay on your medication. Now, I can't say that you're not taking it, I wouldn't know that as a fact. However, these past few months, you've taken a lot of time off. You've missed two important deadlines, and I felt like you weren't one-hundred percent honest with me when you said you couldn't find the email you sent over, like maybe you hadn't finished it on time and were trying to play it off like it disappeared."

"I wasn't lying to you. I haven't told you everything, but my husband and I have been dealing with some issues at home because of our niece moving in with us. We've had a lot of strange occurrences happening."

He pursed his lips and blew a breath out his nose. "The trouble is what happens at home isn't my concern. Now, don't get me wrong, it's not that I don't care about you, but I have to care when you start bringing your personal and home issues into work."

"With all due respect, sir, I have no idea what you're talking about."

"And that's part of the problem. You've been having trouble remembering a lot lately, I've tried to be understanding since you did tell me about your niece. I know that sort of situation can be stressful. But I can't keep letting things slide and last night, you crossed a line that I can't ignore." He leaned back and started clicking away on his computer mouse. "I need you to give me a convincing argument for this and tell me why I'm making a mistake letting you go from the company." He turned the screen in her direction, his email visible on the screen.

She felt numb. "You're firing me?" She stared at his computer while he moved his mouse to an email from her, sent at one in the morning. He clicked on it and what she saw made her want to throw up or pass out, maybe both. The previous night stormed into her head, flashes of the photos she found on Greg's phone played in her head. Martin was scrolling through a seemingly endless slide show of pictures of her, some with clothes, some without. She didn't take these photos, she wasn't sure she would even know how, but it was clearly her. She saw her face, and the body was the same. The biggest problem wasn't the lack of clothing in many of them, it was the sexual suggestive positions. "I...I'm not...I don't know what to say."

Martin closed the email and turned his screen back to him. "At this point, I don't think there is anything you can say. These images are inappropriate and concerning. As much as I appreciate all the work you've done for me over the years, I can't employ someone who would send photos like this. I can't have you working in my office when you are actively disrespecting both my marriage and your own." He leaned back in his chair and rested his hands on the top of his bulging stomach. "I'll need your key."

She stood slowly, afraid her legs wouldn't support her weight. Her vision was blurred and her head pounded. She had to be dreaming. She collected her bag and unhooked the office key from its ring. She walked to his office, slid the key onto the corner of his desk, and left.

Greg sat on the couch in the family room listening to Holly tell her story about Martin firing her. He wanted to interrupt her and tell her it was her fault, but he let her say what she had to.

"And he told me he didn't know if I was taking my medication, but he assumed I wasn't. I don't think that's very fair, do you? He doesn't have any proof."

Greg stared at her, waiting to make sure Holly had finished speaking. "It was only a matter of time before this happened. You had such a good run. As far as the medication goes, the only way he would know that is if you told him. I, however, don't need you to tell me and I do have proof."

Holly squinted. "What are you talking about?"

"I'm telling you I have proof that you haven't been taking your pills. Bonnie called me, told me she's worried about you and said I should keep an eye on you. What I can't seem to understand is why you would put the empty bottle back in the cabinet instead of telling me about it."

She crossed her arms and leaned back in her chair. "Bonnie couldn't have called you. There is such a thing as confidentiality, you know?"

Gregg crossed his arms to match her. "Yeah. And you signed a waiver stating she could call me if she thought you may be harmful to yourself or others. She's worried about you and she's worried about Paige and Lucy, so she made a decision to call and tell me. I looked and found the empty bottle in the cabinet when she said you told her it was in the trash."

"It was in the trash. But I didn't do it. I just...didn't want you to question me or blame me for it. And I forgot about the waiver."

"I didn't. And luckily for us, neither did she. I really don't care what happened to the pills, but you know damn well you can't be alone with Lucy if you don't take them."

"I've been taking them for years and I really don't think I need them anymore."

"Holly? This isn't an option. I know it was rough for you when Lauren passed away, but those pills are the only thing that kept you out of a hospital. Do you really think I'm going to leave you alone with our daughter if you're not taking them? You came after me with a knife. You stabbed me twice before I managed to wrestle it away from you."

Holly hung her head. "I told you I was sorry about that." Her voice sounded like a young child's.

"It's not about being sorry. It's about the fact that you had no idea what you were doing. You were, and are, emotionally fragile and that medication is the only thing that helps you."

# Chapter 29

## She Does Exist

Monica wondered how much time she had left before people started to question whether she was involved or not. She knew from the beginning it was only a matter of time, but she wanted to play it out as long as she was able. She needed to talk to Paige and she couldn't wait hours to hear from her. Monica had to make a decision fast. *Did she leave Paige at Holly's and disappear like she originally planned? Should she go get Paige and bring her home?* As much as she hated to admit it, she missed her. She couldn't help but wonder what her life would be like if she didn't have to worry about Paige anymore. She watched her for so long, for so many years, she wasn't sure she would know what to do without her.

Thankful she had gotten to meet Lucy earlier, she was concerned about whether she would keep their secret. She promised Paige she wouldn't say anything to her parents. Monica told her they were going to play a game and reminded her that she could get in trouble if she told them because she wasn't supposed to talk to strangers. Paige promised again and claimed to be a "super secret keeper." She beamed when she declared herself as such.

After careful consideration, she decided she would just go and get Paige, pretend she had done everything she needed to do, and was there to claim her child. She would do her best to make the visit as quick as she could, like when she dropped her off. She had enough access to Holly's life and thought she could do everything else from afar. Once her mission was complete and she had finally destroyed Holly's life, she would drop Paige off one more time, this time for good.

Greg answered the door and she stumbled back. She didn't expect him to be home this early in the day, but he was easy to manipulate, as she knew, and she was confident she wouldn't have to talk to him for long. Until Lucy ran up to the door and shouted, "Hi, Aunt Monica."

Monica's heart dropped into her stomach. She did have a slight concern about seeing Lucy but hoped their conversation from earlier would still be fresh in her mind. For the first time in her life, Monica was thankful she and Holly were identical twins. If necessary, she could play it off that their appearance made it obvious who she was. She had options, she could have asked Paige to meet her somewhere, but she didn't want to risk Greg and Monica calling the police, thinking Paige had run away or someone had kidnapped her. This was her decision, and despite how fast her heart was racing, she hoped she made the correct one.

Greg gave Monica a cold, questioning look as he held Lucy back with one hand. "Lucy, go play upstairs."

"But I wanna..."

"Now." He growled with such conviction that Lucy cowered before running off to her room.

Monica and Greg stared at each other. Greg has a look of confusion and anger. Monica's face displayed fear and irritation.

Greg broke the silence after a few moments. "Come to see your sister finally?"

She cast her eyes down to the wooden porch. "No. I came to collect my daughter. I'm sure you two are more than sick of her by now."

At least she had the decency to look ashamed, but Greg knew better. It was all an act to make her seem innocent. He knew from personal experience she was a master at making people give her what she wanted. "She's not here and you can't take her. Don't come back again." He stepped back and tried to close the door.

Monica leaped forward and threw out her arm to stop the door from closing. "What do you mean, I can't take her?" She wanted to laugh at how absurd that statement was. "Paige is my daughter. I can take her any time I damn well please."

Greg eased his resistance on the door. "Wrong. You dropped her off here five months ago. No explanation, no time frame for when you would be back. You never once reached out throughout that time to make sure she was okay. We have probably shown her more love, responsibility, and family values in the last few months than you have throughout her entire life. You want her back? You can go to the police, explain the circumstances to them, and let them come get her. No officers, no daughter." With that, he slammed the door in her face and leaned against it. He allowed himself a moment to get his body to relax. He turned around to find Holly and Paige staring at him, wide eyed and mouths agape.

# Chapter 30

## It's a Lose-lose Situation

Greg was unaware that Holly and Paige had come back inside. They were all enjoying lunch in the backyard, taking advantage of the unseasonably warm day. He looked at each of them. Holly had a slack jaw and wide eyes, shocked that Gregg stood up for Paige the way he did. Paige stood completely still, looking like she would burst into sobs at any moment. If he hadn't felt love from their family yet, she was certainly feeling it now. As much as that pleased Greg, he wished she wasn't there to witness him refusing to give her back to her mother. "I do want to talk about this," he scoffed as he brushed past the two of them and made his way to the backyard. He needed some fresh air.

Holly turned to Paige with a sympathetic smile. "I think maybe I should go talk to him first. Are you okay?"

"I'm not really sure, right now." She gave Holly a half-hearted smile and made her way up the stairs.

Holly walked out the back door. She was cautious about approaching Greg. She knew he probably wanted a few minutes to himself, but she also needed him to talk to her, tell her what he was feeling. She couldn't believe his reaction when Monica told him she wanted to bring Paige home with her. If someone had forced her to guess what he would do, she would have said he would have let her go.

She walked to the edge of the patio and watched him. His body language was that of a broken man. His shoulders slumped and he looked shorter than he actually was. He had his head hung and was pacing in a small circle, crossing his arms and then uncrossing them, before crossing them again. She couldn't imagine what he was going through. The past few months had been hard for all of them. There was a lot of blame thrown around, at lot of issues at home and at work, and Paige's presence had been new, fun, and stressful. Watching her husband, she knew he felt something that she couldn't understand. Never would she have guessed that he would close the door in Monica's face, regardless of the reason for her visit. *Had he thought about what he would do ahead of time? What would they do if Monica did come back with the police? Were either of them prepared for the outcome of that?* Holly had secretly wished Monica wouldn't ever come back, not because she wanted Paige to have to go through that kind of heartbreak, but because she genuinely believed she was better off with them. She shook her head to clear her thoughts. She needed to talk to Greg, she just had no idea what to say to him.

She went back inside, poured two glasses of iced tea, and went back out to start the conversation she wasn't sure she wanted to have. Greg turned as she approached and he had a thankful look in his eyes when she held the glass out to him. "Thought you could use a drink."

"Thanks." His mouth curled up in a half-grateful, half-embarrassed smile. "I'm sorry I closed the door in your sister's face. I know how much you want to get reacquainted with her. I just...I don't know what she was thinking. Did she really believe that either of us would just turn Paige over to her after almost six months? That's...she's insane if that's what she thought." He looked like he startled himself by what he said and Holly had to hold back a chuckle. "Would you have let her go?" He looked at the ground where he was digging the toe of his sneaker into the grass. "In hindsight, I guess it's something we should have discussed. We both knew there was a possibility that she would come back."

"No, I...I don't think I would have. But I also don't think I would have had the same courage you did. You know, to demand the police and slam the door in her face. The second part, mainly, because she is my sister and despite everything, I do want a relationship with her. But I can absolutely say, with certainty, that I would never have let Paige walk out the door. I think I would have demanded an explanation of sorts." Holly was relieved Greg had started the discussion. She still didn't know what she would say. "So, what do we do know? Do we talk to Paige and ask what she wants to do? We didn't give her a choice and she's the one stuck in the middle. Should we go to the police before Monica gets a chance to, or should we sit back and wait, see if she really is serious about getting her daughter back?"

Greg saw the frustration on her face, the tension in her muscles. He knew she was fighting a losing battle between her heart and her brain. She wanted what was best for Paige. She also wanted a relationship with her sister. He knew the last thing she wanted to do was cause any more harm or put up another barrier between them. Monica didn't need any more ammunition to hate Holly. "I think, the two of us should take some time to think about what we feel is best. Later tonight, after dinner, we'll talk about it, just the two of us, and we'll see where we are at that point. Tomorrow, we'll have a conversation with Paige." He drew in a deep breath and squared his shoulders. "If Monica happens to show up with the police in the meantime, unfortunately, we won't have a choice."

Paige chose not to come down for dinner that night so Holly left a plate outside her door. Her feelings were conflicting. She felt bad that Greg turned Monica away the way he did, but what did she expect? In everyone's eyes, it looked like she had abandoned her daughter because no one knew the truth. Between Greg, Holly, and Lucy, Paige felt more love than she had her entire life. Greg closing the door in Monica's face was the first time anyone had ever shown her that they cared for her. Because of that, she also felt terrible about what she had done to them. Holly had never done anything to her to deserve what she did. Lucy certainly didn't deserve someone hurting her, and Greg didn't deserve her lying to him. Her brain was telling her not to say anything for fear of getting in trouble and her heart was telling her to march down the stairs and confess everything.

She curled up on her bed, agonizing over whether to tell them or not. She wanted to sneak out of the house and meet Monica but felt, because Holly and Greg had become suspicious, that they would follow her. Instead of leaving, she thought it would be better to lay low for a few days to see if things would blow over. She let her emotions get the better of her and she cried herself to sleep.

In the morning, she awoke with swollen, red eyes and her head was pounding. She should have known not to fall asleep that way. She took a hot shower and made her way down to the kitchen, hoping coffee and some aspirin would make her head feel better. She almost never drank coffee, but Holly would allow it when she had a headache. When she walked in, Greg and Holly were both sitting at the table. "Good morning." She did her best to make her voice sound lighter than she was feeling. They both acknowledged her but only managed half-smiles. They watched as she made her way around the kitchen and it put her nerves on edge. She had a sinking feeling they were waiting for her and she didn't feel it was for a good reason.

Holly broke the silence once Paige sat down. "So, Paige? Something happened yesterday that I wasn't aware of until Greg told me about it and I think we need to discuss it."

All the nerves in her body began buzzing. She had no idea what Holly was talking about. "What did I miss?" She tried to sound innocent, but her voice squeaked, giving her away.

"Well, obviously, you know that Monica, your mother, was here. And I want to come back to this part in a minute, but I have to say, I was a bit surprised that the two of you barely looked at each other. I mean, regardless of what she has done, I would have thought you would have at least had something to say to her, some sort of reaction."

Greg interrupted her with a hand placed gently on her shoulder to guide her back to the real question. "Maybe you should tell her what happened so we can get an answer to that first."

Holly cleared her throat and drew in a deep breath. "Anyway, When Greg answered the door, Lucy ran up and yelled "Hi, Aunt Monica." She let her sentence hang and watched as Paige curled into herself.

Paige could feel the heat rising in her cheeks. *Shit, shit, shit.* She knew she would have to tell the truth; she didn't have a choice now. This day was going to be so much worse than she expected. "I...we..." She burst into tears before she could stop herself.

"I understand that you're upset, Paige. I can't say that I blame you. But we do need to know how Lucy knows who Monica is." Greg spoke gently and with concern.

"That day we went for a walk," she choked out between sobs, "the day you called the police? Lucy met Monica that day. We saw her while we were walking and I introduced them. I didn't have a choice. I couldn't just walk past my own mother and I couldn't stop her from introducing herself to Lucy."

Holly was impressed she was able to come up with such a good excuse in a short amount of time. While she did believe some of it was true, Paige somehow made herself seem like she was the victim. "So, how was Monica that day? Was she happy to see you?"

Paige could feel Holly luring her into a trap that she wouldn't be able to free herself from. *Had Holly spoken to Monica? Did Lucy already tell her what happened that day?* "You probably know Monica better than anyone else, is she ever really happy to see anyone?" She thought, if she could show that she was on holly's side, she might have a better chance of convincing her she was telling the truth.

"Funny, you've been calling her Monica all morning. You also made that same mistake a few weeks ago. What happened to you referring to her as 'my mother?'" Holly was staring at Paige and she could feel her eyes burning into her skin while she waited for a response.

"She practically abandoned me on your doorstep. I may be young but I'm pretty sure that's hardly something a mother would do."

Holly and Greg stared at her with amused expressions on their faces. "Monica isn't actually your mother, is she Paige?"

Paige didn't know why but having Greg doubt what she was saying hurt more than she thought it would. It could be because he was the first decent man she had ever had contact with. Since the day they met, he had always treated her with respect and he had real conversations with her. He never once looked at her as being in the way, an annoyance, or a child who should bring him whatever he wanted. She couldn't bring herself to answer his question. She just sighed and dropped her head toward the table.

No one spoke for a few minutes. Greg finally stood and dumped the remainder of his coffee into the sink before leaving the kitchen. Holly, relieved to have at least one question answered, followed suit.

Paige retreated to her bedroom and heard Holly and Greg leave the house. She was certain they were going to the police station and she didn't know whether to stay and take the blame for all her lies or if she should run. If she chose to run, did she go directly to Monica to warn her, or would that lead the police directly to her? In her mind, she didn't have any safe options.

# Chapter 31

## She was Lost but She Found Herself

She thought about Monica again, about the deal they made. She was beginning to loathe the woman who promised her a place to stay as long as she kept up her end of their deal. If Holly and Greg learned the truth, they would almost certainly kick Paige out of their house. If Monica found out, she would most likely disappear and leave Paige behind for breaking their agreement. Either way, if Paige didn't fix it, she would be on her own again with no place to go.

Feeling she didn't have any other choice, she pulled her backpack from the closet and started stuffing her clothes in it, being sure to take her favorite articles. She didn't waste any time but wasn't as frantic as she was when she did the same thing at her foster mother's house just over a year ago. Before leaving, she stood in the doorway, looking at what she would be leaving behind. Until she moved in here, she had never had a full-sized bed, more than one pillow, or even the luxury of a pillowcase with ruffles on the border. This room alone brought her a comfort she had never known. The family gave her everything she never knew she needed. As mad as she was at Monica, she needed to talk to her, ask her what she was supposed to do.

With apprehension slithering through her veins, she left the house. The weather matched her emotional state. It was colder than she expected and the sky was spitting fat rain drops. *Perfect.* She walked with purpose, weaving through the trees that lined the road. They offered protection from the rain and limited her visibility from cars, specifically Holly and Greg's. She didn't have a plan before she left. As she neared the end of the private road, she decided she would call Monica when she reached the main street.

She stopped. It hit her all at once. If Monica wanted to, she could blame everything on Paige. All she had to do was tell the police she dropped her off at her sister's, but she could blame Paige for everything else and claim she had no idea about any of it. Monica was good at covering her tracks. She never said anything via text that the police could consider concrete evidence and Paige knew she used a prepaid cell phone. She wondered how much the police would be able to figure out, if she had enough evidence against Monica to keep herself out of trouble. She contemplated for a few minutes and made up her mind to stick to her original plan. She needed to talk to Monica.

Back on the move, she dug through the bottom pocket of her bag, looking for her cell when a hand reached out from behind a tree and pulled her back. Paige screamed and swung her arm behind her, her fist connecting with something hard.

"Ow, you bitch."

Paige turned and saw Monica cradling her face in her palm. "Oh, I'm so sorry. I didn't know it was you."

"Is that how you show me you appreciate everything I've done for you? You punched me."

"You scared the shit out of me. I don't walk around expecting someone to jump out and grab me in the middle of the woods. What were you doing?"

"I was waiting for you. I figured it was only a matter of time before you showed your face." She rubbed her hand along her cheek. "Damn, you got me good."

"I was going to go see you. Why didn't you text me?"

"I did, about twenty minutes ago."

"My phone's in my bag." She realized her mistake and curled her lip. "What do you want?"

"Is that any way to talk to your mother? You just said you were coming to see me anyway."

Paige felt unsure of everything all morning and the words that came out of Monica's mouth set her nerves on fire and she started laughing. "That's exactly what I was going to see you about. Greg and Holly asked me this morning if you're really my mother."

Monica stared at Paige with her head tilted and her mouth open. "That's not funny. This is a big problem, Paige."

"They didn't seem to care that much. I think they just want the truth. Holly's really mad though." She pulled her lips between her teeth and her eyes narrowed. "I didn't tell you, but Greg told her he met you a few years ago. He said he found you and tried to convince you to go see Holly and you refused."

"So, they think this is all my fault?" Her shoulders tensed under the sweater she was wearing.

"It came up, but they moved on from it."

"Moved on? What does that mean?"

"Just...they don't know who to blame. Sometimes it's me, sometimes it's you, and sometimes it's Holly. They got into a big fight a couple of weeks ago because she stopped taking her medication and didn't tell anyone."

Monica's eyebrows shot up. "That's the first bit of good news you've brought me. Speaking of, I have some news for you." She closed her eyes and took a deep breath. As soon as she said those words, a rumble of thunder cut across the sky and the rain started coming down in sheets.

Paige's heart rate sped up. She had never witnessed Monica looking uncomfortable and she took notice of the timing of the thunder. "What?"

She took another deep breath. "Well, you know how they asked you if I was your mother?" She cast her eyes down and stared at the blanket of leaves on the ground. "What would you do if you found out I was?" She took a quick glance at Paige before looking at the ground again.

Paige didn't answer her right away, her body frozen in place. Flashes of meeting Monica in random places flickered through her mind, she followed her everywhere for months. Paige didn't think anything of it at the time. "What are you talking about?" She wasn't sure she wanted to hear the answer. Beads of sweat broke out over her entire body despite the rain and freezing wind.

She closed her eyes and shook her head. "I don't know a gentle way to tell you. I am your mother. I gave you up when you were six months old. I thought, at first, that I would be able to care for you but...I just don't have that motherly instinct that Holly has. I knew I wasn't going to be a good mother to you and I wanted better for you."

"Better? Do you have any idea how many foster homes they shuffled me off to when I was young? Everyone I went to was worse than the last. And my last house? The one I destroyed with that fire? During the times my foster mom didn't kick me out and actually allowed me to stay in the house, I had to barricade my bedroom door so her boyfriends couldn't get in in the middle of the night. Do you think you did me a favor?" It was a good thing there weren't any houses around because every word that came out of her mouth got louder.

"You were so young; I thought someone would adopt you, someone who could care for you in a way that I couldn't."

"Well, you were wrong. Why didn't you leave me with Holly then?"

Monica looked at her with tears in her eyes, threatening to spill over. "I couldn't leave you there because I didn't want you growing up with that big of a lie."

# Chapter 32

## Guilty if We're Charged

Greg and Holly arrived at the police station an hour later. They discussed their plan the night before and on the ride in, briefly since Lucy was in the car. They were both shaking with nerves and neither of them knew where they should start once they got there. They didn't have any good options. *Did they start at the beginning with the history between Holly and Monica? Should they begin with Monica dropping Paige on their doorstep? Was their best defense to tell the officers Monica took in a juvenile they don't believe is related to her? Or do they get right to it and tell them they've been housing a teenager they believed was their niece?*

The interview room was freezing and Holly hadn't stopped shivering since she walked in. They spent over three hours trying to make sure they had given the officers as much detail as possible. Holly asked for a cup of coffee to warm her up a bit and was sorry she had after taking the first sip. The room echoed every time someone spoke or shuffled their feet. Greg felt as though they were interrogating him rather than interviewing. The room was empty save for the steel table and four chairs that surrounded it and the cement floor sent a chill through the bottom of his shoes.

Holly went as far back as her and Monica's childhood years to force the officers to understand how bad their relationship was. She needed them to understand what Monica was like and how far she might be willing to go to get revenge against her, even after so many years. They explained the incident with Lucy about the paper she turned into the school saying she wasn't safe as well as the bruise she had woken up with. The officers heard that Paige had taken Lucy to meet Monica without their consent and swore her to secrecy about the meeting. Holly was particularly sensitive to that story because it bothered her so much that Monica tried to meet Lucy without her permission. She assumed Monica wasn't a great mother, but that incident led her to fully believe Paige wasn't her real daughter. No mother would do that to another.

They walked the officers through the issues Holly was having at work with her files disappearing and the photos sent to her boss. They discussed the chat that took place on Holly's computer and ultimately ended up in Greg's email. They both took time explaining why they didn't believe Paige was Monica's real daughter. They wanted it to be clear that Monica led them to believe she was their niece and had no idea, when she moved in, that she may not be related at all. When they spoke about it between themselves, they agreed they would tell the police every detail and not leave anything out. They admitted their faults with their reasoning behind the decisions they made, such as not enrolling Paige in school, hoping no one would hold those decisions against them. Neither of them knew what kind of laws were in place for a situation like this.

The officers followed them back to their house, hoping to speak to Paige when they arrived. They hoped, since Greg and Holly had already spoken to them, she might be willing to tell them the truth. After living with them so long, they assumed she had developed some emotional attachment to them and were prepared to use that as leverage to get the information they needed. When they arrived, they found the house completely empty. Holly looked around Paige's room and noticed she had packed most of her clothes, her tote bag and backpack were gone, and she had taken a blanket from her bed. Holly was devastated when she realized Paige left and had no intention of returning.

The police assured them before they left the station, they had put a search out for Monica's current residence and were trying to find any motor vehicle information for her. Greg had to admit at that point that he had tried that years ago with no luck. He was only able to find her through a private investigator because she knew how to cover her tracks. They made note of that and moved on to the next step, asking to see both Paige's room and Holly's office. Paige's room was all but empty, as Holly told them. She didn't have much by way of toys or pictures and everything she took was easy to carry in a bag.

Holly's office was a different story. On one picture frame that hung on the wall, they found a small camera placed in the corner, aimed directly at the keyboard on her computer. It was obvious that was how someone got her passwords. A second camera hung on the light directly above her computer which allowed whoever was watching her to see her computer screen. The officers called in a crime scene unit to collect anything they found in the office, and anything remaining in Paige's room.

Before they left, the officers had one last request and it made Greg and Holly cringe. Since Paige wasn't there for them to question, they asked to speak to Lucy instead.

# Chapter 33

## The Truth Does Not Set You Free

For the second time, Greg hired a private investigator to find Monica. They hadn't heard from her since the day she showed up to get Paige and the police hadn't been able to find her. It only took two days to receive her address and Greg was surprised to find she lived in the next town over. The first time he met her, he was unsure of himself but this time, he had good reason to approach her and he wouldn't back down until she told him the truth.

He knocked on the door, not surprised she was living in another trailer park. He pounded his fist on the door, loud enough for all the neighbors to hear. When she opened the door, he pushed past her, accidentally knocking into her shoulder, without waiting for an invitation to come in. "How long were you going to wait to tell me? Were you even planning on telling me or was it a game to you to see how long it would take?"

Monica watched spit fly from his mouth, the reflection caught in the one narrow stream of light her trailer afforded her. "I hope it didn't take you this long to figure out."

"That doesn't answer my question."

"I wasn't purposely keeping it from you if that's what you're implying. I honestly thought you would have figured it out the second you saw her. She looks exactly like Lauren and nothing like Lucy." She waited for a reaction that he didn't give her. "Please, please tell me you've figured that part out."

Greg rolled his eyes to the ceiling. "Years ago."

"Hmm. Does she know you know?"

"I never said anything to her. You know she can't watch Lucy by herself. If she takes her medication late or forgets to take it, I can't risk that."

Monica sat on the arm of the couch; her arms crossed in front of her. "Lucy isn't your responsibility."

Greg shook his head. "Not legally, but I love my daughter."

Monica's eyebrows shot up and one corner of her mouth curled. "Which one?"

He felt like someone punched him in the stomach. "That's not fair. I chose to raise Lucy as my own. You didn't give me that option with Paige. For fifteen years you kept her a secret from me."

"I kept it a secret from her for fifteen years."

For the first time, Greg noticed how cold her eyes are. "That makes it so much worse. Do you have any idea what kind of hell you put that girl through? You should have told me years ago; I would have taken her if you couldn't keep her."

"Wait." Monica stood and started pacing the living room floor. "Did she tell..."

"Yes. Of course, she told me. After you two met up the other day, she told me everything. Thankfully, she was smart enough to come find me without Holly being there. I still haven't figured out how to tell her."

"That little bitch. I can't believe she sold me out. But," she shrugged, "I guess I can't really blame her for wanting to know both her parents after so many years."

"You really don't feel bad at all do you? Not for me, not for her, not for what you put our family through. I missed fifteen years of this girl's life because you wanted to be a selfish, fucking bitch. Getting back at Holly was all you cared about. So what's your plan now that I know? Are you just going to disappear from Paige's life and pretend she doesn't exist?"

"You know? I'm not much of a planner. I mean, aside from all of this. I think I'm going to go back to seeing where each day takes me." She settled on a stool at the kitchen counter. "But, hey, since you're here...what do you say? Wanna check out my bed for old time's sake?"

# Chapter 34

## All the Cards

Monica knocked on the front door hoping they were all home. Greg answered the door and, this time, invited her in, leading her to the family room where everyone was sitting together. He didn't ask what she wanted, he hoped she was there to tell the truth.

Holly's heart jumped when she saw her before the anger took over. "I thought Greg told you we'll only let her go if you bring the police with you."

"I'm not here to take Paige. I'm here to make sure he told you the truth."

Holly stood so her sister wouldn't have the advantage. "Which one? Was he supposed to tell me about meeting you years ago? Did you want him to admit that he was sleeping with you? Or are you looking for the full confession that he fathered your child?"

Greg gasped and his jaw dropped open. "How do you know about that?"

Holly glanced in his direction and he saw the same coldness in her eyes that he saw in Monica's the day before. "Seriously? How wouldn't I know? The first thing I noticed about Paige was that her and Lauren could have been twins. They look exactly alike. Which, considering Monica and I are twins, would make sense. The problem is, Lauren didn't look like me and Paige doesn't either. They both look exactly like you."

"Holly, I..."

"Nope. You don't get to say anything. You lied to me. You cheated on me and had a child with my sister."

"Mommy?"

"Lucy, go to your room, now."

She scrambled to her feet and ran up the stairs.

Monica smiled at both of them. "Well, I think this is your chance, Greg. Here's your opportunity to tell her you know she cheated on you, too, and someone else fathered her child. You know, the one you've been raising for the past nine years." She had a wicked grin on her face.

Greg stood and walked toward the door. This wasn't the truth he was expecting. He held it open for Monica. "I think you need to leave. Now."

Two

Years

Later

# Epilogue

## The Aftermath

Paige sat at the kitchen table, working on her schoolwork. She missed so much school over the years, Greg took it upon himself to enroll her in night school rather than have her go through a multitude of tests to see which grade level she would fit in. It had been just the two of them for the past eighteen months and they were happier than they had been in years. For Paige's sixteenth birthday, they took a trip to the Bahamas. Greg knew he wouldn't be able to make up for the first seventeen years of her life, but he was determined to make the next seventeen as memorable as he could.

Holly and Monica started speaking again. Their relationship was still strained but they would get together for lunch or have a picnic with Lucy once a month. Monica was beginning to feel bad about all the stuff she did to her sister. Now that they were both adults, she realized her hatred toward her was nothing more than a childhood rivalry. Holly, happy to have her sister in her life again, was learning all she could about her. It would take some time, but it would be worth it. Her sister had ruined her marriage and if she played her cards right, Holly would taste the sweetest revenge.

# Author's Bio

Trish recently moved across the country where she found her forever home, enjoying the desert sunshine and wildlife all year long. She was born and raised in a small town in northern Connecticut. Growing up, she was always fascinated by unsolved mysteries and true crimes as well as the psychological elements behind them. As an avid reader, her go to books are thriller/suspense, true crime, and cozy mysteries.

# Author's Note

When you are finished reading, if you do not keep physical books, please consider donating your copy to your local library for their book sale or to your local prison book program.